Mail Order Susanna

Book Three of
Sweet Willow Mail Order Brides

Charlotte Dearing

This is a clean, wholesome love story set in late 19th century Texas. Love conquers all.

Chapter One

Susanna Astor

Aunt Molly's letters were usually fun to read, filled with stories about neighbors and their children, silly things to make Susanna laugh. This letter was different, though. She could almost hear the strain in Molly's voice, coming off the written page.

Susanna desperately wanted to know the source of Molly's indignation, but Molly was not one to leave out her own feelings. The first two pages made it very clear how Molly would not stand for what had happened, whatever it was, and that she was already making plans to disrupt the whole affair.

On page three, Susanna finally gathered that Molly's anger stemmed from a tea party conversation involving a wedding announcement.

Susanna flipped to the fourth and final page.

I almost fainted when I learned of your engagement to Edgar Wiggins...

Susanna gasped and sank to the edge of the settee. A stack of books slid off the nearby cushion, tumbling to the floor.

You cannot possibly marry that horrid man. I will not allow it. He's been married twice and both wives died under mysterious circumstances.

I insist you come to lunch to discuss this disgraceful matter. Shall we say Tuesday noon? Did I mention I have a new parrot? I'm teaching Dimitri to insult your insufferable father. He'll be the star of my next garden party. (Dimitri, that is. Not your father.)

Aunt Molly despised Susanna's father. She claimed her beloved sister, Martha, had made a disastrous choice when she married Hubert Astor. With her mother's death, Molly had taken a brief pause from her outward disdain for Susanna's father. Very brief.

When you come for lunch, I shall tell you about a grand scheme I have for you. I intend to help you find a husband. He won't be anyone like Edgar Wiggins. In fact, it won't be anyone in Albany.

A scheme. Molly always had a grand scheme.

With growing panic, Susanna returned to Molly's news about the engagement to Edgar Wiggins. Susanna shook her head, refusing to believe the words. They had to be simple, groundless rumors. A mistake. Or a misunderstanding of some sort.

Perhaps Molly had indulged in a little too much sherry at the tea party. After all, Aunt Molly rarely went to tea parties to drink tea.

Susanna needed to ask her father. If she caught him in a decent mood, he could explain everything. Edgar Wiggins was his new business partner.

Her chest tightened. She and her father rarely spoke. He was easily angered. Especially by her. It had been that way ever since Susanna's mother died.

As her worry grew, like vines wrapping around her heart, she thought of Henry. Her ally. Her friend. Her only confidante.

Dear, sweet-natured Henry. He'd served the family forever, it seemed, but to Susanna he was much more than a butler. Henry was like a kindly grandfather, wise friend, and trusted counselor all in one. While Aunt Molly could always conjure up an outlandish scheme, Henry always weighed in with the voice of reason.

He cared for her as if she were his own child.

When young, she had been frail and sickly. It was Henry who called the doctor, Henry who organized round-the-clock bedside watches, Henry who paced the hall outside her room as she drifted in and out of restless sleep.

Henry would know what to do.

She went to the foyer to speak to a servant. "Rosalind, please ask Henry to come."

Returning to the parlor, she searched the room for her gardening gloves. The tips protruded from a stack of books on a nearby table. She moved them aside, causing several books to tumble from the stack.

She glanced around the cluttered room, searching for her rose shears, spying them on the floor by a Dickens novel. She snatched them and hurried to the garden terrace.

The morning sun warmed her shoulders as she crossed the terrace to the rose bushes. The fragrance of the Damask roses reminded Susanna of her mother, the only memories that had not faded over the years. The soft perfume of the delicate flowers made her smile. She could almost hear her mother singing an old French hymn.

Alone in the garden, Susanna sang what little she remembered of the song as she cut the roses. She snipped the stem of one final rose, tucked it with the other blooms and crossed the sun-dappled terrace. When she stepped inside, she found Henry waiting.

"Good morning." Glancing at the open window, she wondered if he'd heard her singing. "How long have you been here?"

"A moment or two."

He stood by the doorway, his back ramrod. Despite the years, he still had his military bearing. She could not remember a single day of her life without Henry. In all her nineteen years, she'd never seen him unkept or rumpled or, God forbid, messy.

She searched his face for a sign that he might know something about Molly's letter. His expression was stoic, as always, one that told her nothing. In the bright sunshine, she noted the deep lines on his forehead.

He looked older. Tired. Haggard.

A pang of guilt stabbed her heart. She rarely thought about Henry's advanced years. He could have retired years ago but stayed on at the Astor home to care for her. Not that he ever said as much.

In less than two years, she would come into her inheritance. While she had no idea how much money she would receive, she intended to do something for Henry. She'd send him somewhere warm, perhaps to the hot springs in the South. The warm mineral waters would ease his rheumatism.

Despite his tired expression, he was immaculate. His suit was cleaned and pressed, his starched shirt as white as new snow. His shoes gleamed with a perfect polish. Not a single speck of lint dared cling to the fabric of Henry's perfect attire.

A sudden urge came over her. She wanted to rush to him and weep and tell him every one of her fears. He would be shocked. Utterly dismayed. While he was the kindest person she knew, he kept everyone, her included, at an arm's length.

"I gathered roses." She held up the straggling bouquet. "Mother's Damask roses."

"Your father is waiting to speak to you."

She drew a sharp breath of surprise. Her intention was to approach her father and find out more. But Father was waiting to speak to *her*.

Cold dread tightened across her shoulders. She pushed away the panic. Fear made her stutter, and her stutter always sent her father into a dark, terrifying rage. She needed to compose herself. She needed a moment to calm the turmoil of her thoughts. If she could only keep her fear at bay, she could find out if Molly was right.

Her heart thundered against her ribs. She drew a deep breath, took a vase from the cupboard, and set it on a sunny spot near the window. Henry sighed, crossed the room and took the vase from her. He returned a moment later with the container filled with clean water.

He cleared his throat. "I will arrange the flowers while you speak with Mr. Astor. I promise to snip all the thorns."

Susanna was not ready. Her hands trembled. She clenched her fingers, trying to tamp down her worry. "Did you know the Damask rose came from Damascus?"

His brows lifted. His lips quirked with the merest hint of a smile. "I did not."

"I'm surprised. You always know the history of Mother's roses."

She went on before he could speak. "The Damask rose was brought to Europe in the thirteenth century. It might surprise you to learn by whom."

"Indeed." He tugged a watch from his pocket, checked the time and snapped it shut.

"Robert de Brie brought the rose to Europe. A Frenchman. That's not the surprising part. The surprising part is that he was a Crusader."

"Astonishing."

She turned back to the flowers and snipped another rose. "I wonder if Mother knew. She would have enjoyed the story of a knight journeying home with roses. I wonder if Sir Robert had a ladylove. Perhaps the rose reminded him of his sweetheart, waiting for him."

Henry said nothing, refusing to indulge in a conversation while her father waited.

Attempting to draw him into a different subject, she glanced at him with a sheepish smile. "Did you hear me just now when I was in the garden?"

"Singing?"

"Yes. Singing."

"I did."

She winced.

As a child, Susanna knew that many people hoped she had inherited her mother's voice. The years of music classes made one thing abundantly clear – talent often skipped generations. People always seemed so disappointed, her father, his friends, even Aunt Molly.

Their disappointment pained her, especially when it was Henry who heard her sing.

Many years ago, he'd worked for her mother's family, when her mother was just a child. He knew firsthand that Susanna's mother had the voice of an angel. He also knew how awful Susanna sounded in comparison.

Henry never let her wallow in self-pity. His remedy was to tease her about her singing which, oddly, made her laugh and feel a little better. Good old Henry.

"And did I remind you of a meadowlark?" She schooled her features to suppress a smile as she snipped a few more thorns.

"Yes," he said absently. "I felt certain the divine sound came from a meadowlark on a summer morning."

She set the shears aside and tugged off her gloves. "Well, that's worrisome. Usually, you tell me my singing sounds like a scalded cat. Or another animal suffering the throes of a gruesome and prolonged death. Not a meadowlark."

He frowned at his lapse.

"You're worried about my meeting with Father. That's why you're saying nice things about my singing. Out of pity."

"You must go speak to your father. This is not a matter which can wait."

A coil of fear tightened around her heart. Dear heavens. This could only mean one thing – Molly's outlandish words about an engagement were true.

"I believe your father would like to see you married to Mr. Wiggins."

Her heart thudded. There it was. Henry said the words matter-of-factly, leaving out the sordid details about what must have happened. Father intended to marry her off. He'd wash his hands of his daughter. Mr. Wiggins would get a third wife along with her inheritance.

Susanna straightened her shoulders as she turned to Henry. "What will I do if he insists on marrying me off?"

The color drained from Henry's face. After a moment, he answered carefully. "You have every right to reject an offer from Mr. Wiggins."

"How can I confront a man who despises me?" she whispered.

"You cannot turn from your problems, my dear," Henry said gently. "I will help you in any way I can, but you are the only one who can address this trouble."

There was a knock at the door. A servant appeared. "Your father will speak to you, Miss Astor."

With a heavy heart, Susanna left the parlor, Henry trailing a half-step behind. Their footsteps echoed down the marble hallway. She shivered from the chill. The cold seemed to seep from the walls. The house was like a mausoleum, a shrine to the Astor family. The oil paintings seemed even more ominous than usual. Dark, scowling figures from the past, minor political leaders, forgotten military men, brandishing swords, or astride prancing horses.

The paintings served as a reminder.

She'd failed. She'd failed by being an only child, and worse, a girl. She had none of her mother's gifts for music or poise or charm. What good was a girl with no talents, who grew bored with dances and tea parties, an awkward girl who always had her nose in a book? A girl who stuttered when nervous?

As they neared the study, Henry spoke. "Susanna, your mother was formidable. She sang in opera houses all over Europe. She performed for royalty. You are her precious child, the daughter she loved. When you turn twenty-one, you will inherit your grandfather's fortune. Your father won't control the purse strings anymore. Until then, you must assert yourself."

Her eyes stung. A wave of emotions washed over her. She wished she could run away or be anywhere other than standing at her father's door.

Henry went on, a slight smile tugging at his lips. "As you know, I depend upon your inheritance. The instant you become an heiress, I intend to give my notice."

She offered a half-hearted smile.

Her inheritance was a long-standing joke. Henry had remained in the Astor home despite the family's money troubles. Over the years he'd been offered other jobs with better pay. He'd stayed on at the Astor home to watch over her, Susanna knew.

He clasped his hands behind his back, speaking in a solemn tone but with a faint twinkle in his eye. "I will leave my position as your butler and secretary and all the other roles I perform flawlessly and with complete devotion."

"I know, Henry. And when I come into my inheritance, I will be sure to hire a butler and secretary for *you*."

"A dozen of both."

"Of course."

He lowered his voice to a conspiratorial whisper. "And don't forget the pastry chef."

"Pastry chef?"

"From Paris."

"If you insist. I thought you didn't indulge in sweets."

"I intend to begin the moment you come into your fortune."

"Indeed?" she said, mimicking him.

"You owe me a great deal for all the times I read *The Nutcracker and the Mouse King*." He straightened and gave her a stern, albeit mocking look. "If you won't confront your father for your sake, at least do it for poor, old Henry."

"All right. Thank you." Overcome with emotion and with gratitude, she blinked back tears that threatened to fall and gave a deep sigh. "Do you know how much I adore you?"

He pretended to grimace, but the slight quirk of his lips betrayed his delight at her rare words of affection. He waved a dismissive hand, shooing her toward the door of her father's office.

Chapter Two

Beau Bailey

The surgeon tugged the stained shirt from Beau's shoulder to examine the wound. The shirt had a hole blasted front and back. Beau eyed the shirt with some regret. It was one more shirt that needed mending.

The surgeon searched for the bullet, probing Beau's side while he grumbled.

"It's just a scratch," Beau said. "I told you, it's nothing. My danged shirt is in worse shape than me."

"Sit tight, Bailey," Captain Reynolds, his commanding officer, ordered. "Let the doc do his work."

The doctor grumbled under his breath, probably irritated that Beau had been right after all. The bullet had passed clean through just below his ribs. Thankfully, it had missed the lung.

A few hours earlier, Beau had collared the criminal and delivered him to the sheriff. The man was wanted in three states for robbery. During the skirmish, the man had fired a few shots, and, unfortunately, the last bullet had pierced Beau's side. Aggravating, but part of the job.

Captain Reynolds liked to joke that Beau, like a cat, had nine lives. Despite that, Reynolds didn't take kindly to Beau's habit of refusing to see a doc. In the past, Beau ignored his commanding officer's request. He didn't want a sawbones to fuss over him. This time, Reynolds didn't bother giving a direct order. Reynolds just hauled Beau to the doc's office himself.

Reynolds stood a few paces away from the examining table. They peered at Beau's side where the bullet entered his chest and noted the matching spot on his back.

Captain Reynolds gave a low whistle.

The doc shook his head with disbelief. "It didn't hit his lungs."

"Isn't that what I told you?" Beau asked.

Captain Reynolds folded his arms across his chest. "So now you're a doctor?"

"It's not hard to figure out a man's taken a bullet to the lung." Beau muttered. "I knew as soon as Roberts shot me, he'd missed."

The captain arched a disbelieving brow.

Beau went on. "I didn't even notice the bullet till Captain Reynolds griped about me making a mess."

"A mess?" the doc asked.

"Just a little blood in the captain's office." Beau shrugged.

"I just had the floors mopped," Reynolds snapped. "It seems a man would know if he'd been shot."

Beau shook his head. "It was just a .22. And it only grazed my side. If it had hit my lung, I'd be coughing blood."

The doc nodded. "He's right. Plenty of blood but not too serious."

The captain eyed Beau's shoulder. "What happened there?"

Beau glanced at the injury he'd gotten a couple of months back. "I got the business end of a Bowie knife."

The captain sighed wearily. He'd given up keeping track of Beau's near-death incidents, or making comments about using up some of his lives.

Beau dragged his palm over his jaw. He had a sizeable scar trailing across his mouth and jaw from another knife fight. He liked to joke that the knife scar ruined his good side. It didn't compare to the scars he'd gotten in a fire last year in a hotel in Waco.

The right side of his face and neck and his right shoulder were disfigured from the blaze. The scars were gruesome. People grimaced when they saw him. Beau still dreamed of the terrible fire. A blaze was worse than a bullet. He knew that firsthand.

The doctor dabbed Beau's wound with antiseptic. The man would probably wrap a bandage around his chest and give him firm instructions to rest for a few weeks.

The doc gestured for Beau to lift his arms so he could wrap the bandage around his chest. Captain Reynolds watched intently, probably waiting for Beau to grimace with pain.

"I'm fine," Beau said. "More than fine. I'd like my next assignment, sir. I'm requesting permission to transfer east. Houston. I aim to bring in the Craddick brothers."

Captain Reynolds knit his brow as he mulled over Beau's words. "The governor expects you in Austin."

The doctor gave Beau a pointed look. "Really? The governor?"

Beau shrugged a shoulder. "He wants to give me a commendation and shake my hand or whatever they do at these shindigs."

"Sounds right fine," the doc said. "You could use a few days of rest and recovery."

"That's what I thought," Captain Reynolds said. "Not to mention you'd do well to lie low for a while."

The doc paused his bandaging and gave Beau another inquisitive look. "What now?"

Beau grimaced, wishing he could just be done with the chit-chat. "Some newspaper man in Fort Worth wrote a story about me. He called me the Lone Lawman and went on about my bringing in three bank robbers in Abilene."

Irritation burned inside his chest. The three men were a dangerous bunch of outlaws. It was gratifying to bring an end to their violence. That was what made the job worth doing. Adding three men to his tally of arrests hadn't hurt his feelings either. But then things got out of hand. The notoriety of the criminals, and especially the story of their arrest, drew a bunch of nosy newspaper men.

The writer from Fort Worth had gone on about Beau's appearance. He'd written that "Beau" meant handsome in French and that the first thing anyone noticed about Beau Bailey was his scars, not his good looks. The writer probably thought he was being funny. Beau didn't care much. The main problem was that his scars made it hard to blend in with regular folk, which could be important on some missions as a Ranger.

Beau would have liked to forget about the whole newspaper debacle. Not Reynolds. His commanding officer seemed to take the entire matter personally. He could see Reynolds getting riled up all over again.

Captain Reynolds grew red-faced. "Dang the Fort Worth paper. The fool newsboy wrote about Bailey's scars, his eye color. Then he had to tell about the ambush and arrest. Now half the outlaws in Texas are on the lookout for a green-eyed Ranger with a few scars."

Beau grimaced. He hoped the captain was wrong. Hopefully, people would forget the story sooner rather than later.

The captain went on. "The reporter had to jaw about Beau's height and build. Might as well have painted a target on the back of Beau Bailey."

"I ain't worried about it," Beau said. "People will forget about all that soon enough. I just want to start looking for the Craddick brothers. Even if it means riding a train instead of a horse."

The doctor shook his head and resumed bandaging Beau's midsection. "I heard about the Craddick brothers. Can't recall why. Maybe gambling halls."

"They started out with card games, but they've moved on to trains." Beau clenched his jaw. "They prey on women traveling alone."

More than anything, Beau despised criminals who stalked vulnerable women. His father and grandfather before him liked to talk about the family creed of "serve and protect," a sentiment that the Bailey men felt in their very souls. His grandfather and father had both been widowed early in life, their wives lost to accidents, not violence, but both carried sorrow and guilt for the rest of their lives.

Beau had resolved long ago that he'd live his life as a bachelor. His only family, cousins Seth and Noah, liked to joke that Beau was wedded to his work. Beau never argued that point. Life was simpler as a bachelor, and as a Ranger. He could keep his eye fixed firmly on criminals.

Now, it was time to stop the Craddick brothers.

He'd read the reports of the robberies. The Craddick brothers were more than simple thieves. They were vicious and violent outlaws.

Beau turned his attention to his commanding officer. "With your permission, sir, I'd like to transfer to Houston."

"You think you're ready?" Captain Reynolds asked. "You got shot two hours ago."

"I'm ready, sir."

"I hate to lose you, Bailey. Ever since you came to West Texas, our regular outlaws have hightailed it. Things are almost quiet around these parts."

The doc snorted. He sighed and frowned at Beau's bandage and continued with his task without further commentary.

Beau dismissed the captain's praise. "I don't want any more womenfolk getting robbed or injured. Or worse."

Reynold's shrugged. "Sounds like you've made up your mind. I'll send a telegram to my counterpart in Houston to let him know to expect you."

"Much obliged."

"You realize you'll be working under Captain Maddox?"

Beau didn't realize his commanding officer would be Captain Maddox. He'd have to keep that in mind. Working with Maddox would be a little trickier than working under Captain Reynolds, but Beau was ready for a change of action. He'd grown tired of the dusty border town. Staying in one place made him restless.

When the doc finished, Beau got to his feet and put on his shirt, ignoring the torn, soiled fabric. The tight bandages bothered him more than anything. First chance he got, he intended to tear them off. He made a point of thanking the surgeon for his care as he put on his worn Stetson. "Guess this is the last time I'll be seeing you, doc."

"Shucks," the doc drawled.

"Got to keep moving."

The doc looked resigned. "You're leaving the fine town of Hell Paso?"

Beau grinned. "Yessir. It's time to go. I'm not a man who can settle in one spot for too long."

I

Chapter Three

Susanna

Susanna awoke to find herself in an unfamiliar bed. She sat bolt upright and looked around in bewilderment. Slowly, it dawned on her. She was in Aunt Molly's guest room.

Her memory of last night was hazy. Dressing hastily, she tried to piece together the events of the prior evening. She recalled meeting with her father, how he'd announced that she would marry Edgar Wiggins. He alluded to a debt he owed the man, a debt she would need to repay. If she refused, he'd disown her.

She argued. More accurately, she tried to argue. Her words became twisted. And then the worst happened.

She stuttered.

When she tripped over her own words, her father flew into a rage. He shouted the most appalling things that Susanna had ever heard him say. *Edgar Wiggins will propose. I demand that you accept. Don't you dare humiliate the Astor name...*

The memory slowly returned. She'd fainted. Her father's rampage had been too much. She'd never fainted before, and the mere idea of collapsing while in the same room as her father made her feel even more vulnerable.

Thank goodness for Henry's help. He came to her side, suddenly appearing as she crumpled to the floor. She faintly recalled his instructions to the servants. They'd carried her out of the study, but instead of taking her to her room, they took her to a waiting carriage.

With a heavy heart, she continued dressing in last night's frock. She arranged her hair somewhat respectably, then she slowly went downstairs. Molly played the piano, filling the grand house with music.

Molly stopped playing when Susanna entered the room. "Darling! You're awake! You must be famished. Shall I send for breakfast?"

Without the music, the elegant room filled with chirps and peeps, the morning greetings of Molly's menagerie. Molly kept various birds in her music room and other creatures wandered the gardens behind the house. A peacock squawked on the lawn. A pair of goats grazed on the topiary. A mother duck and her brood waddled past the windows, heading to the fountain.

Molly came to her side and kissed her cheek. She cupped her shoulders and gave her a long, tender gaze before folding her into a warm embrace. "Poor dear," she murmured. "You poor, poor dear."

Susanna knew she should feel heavy, impending doom. Her father had given her an ultimatum. Despite her troubles, she objected to Molly's dire words. Surely things weren't so grim, were they?

Molly relished a dilemma. "Head down and through!" she always cheered. And yes, Henry often commented that Molly was an unbalanced woman, but her relentless optimism always boosted Susanna's morale.

Molly kept her close, refusing to let go. She patted Susanna's shoulder and soothed her with kind words. Susanna clung to the hope that Molly would explain that everything would be fine. Just fine.

A thought came to her. Were things worse than she'd imagined?

"Is one of us gravely ill?" Susanna asked, attempting to make light of the situation.

"No, you saucy girl. Can't I embrace my favorite niece?"

"I'm your only niece."

Molly released her and gave her a look of mild reproach. "I hardly see you anymore. I'm glad you've come for a visit, despite the circumstances."

She rang a bell. In seconds a servant appeared and Molly requested a breakfast tray.

"I hardly remember coming here last night," Susanna said as she studied a large parrot, Molly's latest addition. The bird studied her back, peering at her from his perch.

"Henry brought you," Molly said. "He said your father was in a rage and he had concerns about your safety. I'm sure your father will dismiss him for interfering. He's never cared for Henry."

Susanna doubted that very much. Henry ran the Astor house with military precision. Her father would never find another Henry. Nor would she. Her mind wandered to Mr. Wiggins. What would happen when she had to marry her father's business partner? Mr. Wiggins might not view Henry with quite the same pragmatism.

The parrot fluttered his wings against the bars of the cage. Susanna startled. Feathers fell from his wings. Brilliant blue, the delicate wisps drifted to the bottom of the enormous cage. The bird blinked several times, looking glum. Maybe that was how all parrots looked.

"Dimitri," Molly said in a sing-song voice, crossing the room to the cage. "Dimitri. Pretty boy."

The bird gazed silently.

"Hubert is a vile beast." Molly prompted in the same high-pitched tone.

Dimitri said nothing.

"Go on, pretty Dimitri," Molly urged. "Hubert is a cad."

The bird ruffled his feathers, cocked his head, and warbled. His indistinct response sounded nothing like Molly's suggestions. The bird sounded as if he had a sore throat.

The pitiful noise made Molly draw back with dismay. "They promised me he'd talk. Why won't he talk?"

Distress weighed heavily on Susanna's shoulders. The bird seemed every bit as sad as she was. "He seems sad. You shouldn't keep them in cages."

Molly's jaw dropped. She did not reply. Only a few small cheeps from the other birds filled the silence of the room. Molly blinked several times, her eyes wide.

"What?" Molly asked softly, her tone wounded. "What did you say?"

Susanna shook her head. "I pity any creature kept in a cage."

She had never spoken to her aunt in such a way. Molly had always been a mix of mother and sister to Susanna. On one hand, she was kind and maternal. On the other hand, she was girlish and quick to laugh.

Molly lifted her chin. "I take excellent care of my pets, I will have you know. I get the very best of everything. Dimitri's cage is made of the finest materials."

She turned away, her skirts rustling. There was nothing more to discuss.

Like Molly's pets, Susanna had grown up with fine things. Admittedly, the luxuries had grown fewer and further between, but still. She knew all about extravagances. She wanted to argue the point that no matter how elegant and tasteful the cage, it is still a cage, but suddenly she felt too tired to argue anything.

Besides, Molly looked hurt. She'd never had children of her own. Perhaps that was the reason she doted on the animals, especially the birds. She liked to say that almost nothing made her happier than the sight of a bird and each one was more beautiful than the next.

Susanna admired them too. They were very pretty, and usually seemed happy, but Susanna was sure they would be even prettier if they could spread their wings and fly.

Susanna wandered to the window. Gardeners trimmed hedges and weeded flower plots. Molly's garden was a profusion of blooms and color, the last burst of life before summer ended. Soon the north winds would blow, causing the bright blooms to wither and die. In the past, the gardens delighted Susanna. This morning, they hardly stirred any emotion in her heart other than defeat.

"I'd never seen my father so angry," she said quietly. "He shouted awful things at me."

"He's a beast. A heartless beast. He treated my poor sister abominably. Poor Martha."

"He said that after I married, he never wanted to see my face again."

Molly made a soft, sympathetic sound.

"I told him that escaping his home would be a relief." Susanna turned to face Molly. "I've never said anything so hateful in my life. What if deep down, I'm no better than my father?"

"Don't be absurd. You, my love, are your mother through and through. That's why your father treats you poorly. He never felt worthy of Martha. You are kind. Beautiful.

Thoughtful. And he is vile. Unkind and ugly, both inside and out."

Susanna didn't tell Molly anymore of the meeting last night. She did not want to describe her father's outburst, how he'd broken things as he raged. How she'd stuttered and made him even more angry. How Henry had rushed in just as she was about to faint. There was no telling what might have happened if Henry hadn't stepped into her father's study just as her world fell to pieces.

Her father's final words rung in her ears. *Get her out of my sight.* Susanna cringed at the memory.

"You must leave Albany," Molly said.

"What?"

"It's the only way. If you don't leave, Henry won't either. You know how devoted he is to you."

Susanna rubbed her forehead.

Molly sat on the chesterfield and patted the cushion beside her. "Come sit down. I want to tell you of my scheme."

Susanna did as Molly bid her.

Molly smiled. "I've taken the liberty of speaking to a matchmaking agency again."

"Molly, please. Now's not the time. I've told you I won't marry a stranger."

"I know. And there was a time when I understood your hesitation. But things have taken on a new urgency. In the past, I felt certain you could simply move far away to escape your father, but things have changed. You must leave Albany and then marry. Otherwise, your father will try to marry you off to one of his drinking friends."

Susanna shook her head. "Father has set a date for the wedding, but it's still two months off. I simply need to convince Mr. Wiggins we're not compatible. I'll let him argue the matter with Father. And after that I will petition the holding agency for my inheritance. You see? I have a plan too. And once I have my inheritance, I can help Henry."

Molly paid her no mind and waved an envelope. "This man owns a saloon in Colorado."

"What's a saloon?"

Molly chuckled. "Oh, my dear girl. You see, this is why you should set your books aside every so often. A saloon is a place where they serve spirits. This man won't do at all."

"Because he owns a saloon?"

"Because I've discerned that he only serves whiskey." She wrinkled her nose and tossed the envelope aside. "He might have a little promise if he served something better. Champagne, for example."

Taking the next envelope, she went on. "And this man owns a bookshop in California, which I'm certain appeals to you, my darling little bookworm. However, he lives in a *single* room at the back of the shop. It sounds dreadful. Like a garret of some sort. Clearly Mr. Jones can't possibly afford your reading habits. Why, he'd be out of business in the blink of an eye."

Molly laughed, amused by her own joke.

The servant delivered a breakfast tray and set it on a nearby table. Susanna had no appetite but poured a cup of tea. She offered one to Molly, but her aunt was too absorbed with the letters.

Molly sorted through the stack, muttering to herself as she perused each envelope. When she got to the final envelope, she batted her lashes. "I saved the best for last. This Texas gentleman is quite elderly, and you know I have a fondness for older husbands, especially if they are well-off. It's nice if they're in poor health too. Mr. Robert Anderson is old and rich.

25

He has no children, thankfully, and wants only a marriage of convenience."

"I'm not marrying. Not Mr. Wiggins. And not elderly, childless, and convenient Mr. Anderson in Texas. I'm going to take my inheritance and share it with Henry."

Molly scoffed. "You need to consider Mr. Anderson. It's important to secure a proxy marriage."

Susanna gasped. *"Proxy* marriage? Have you taken leave of your senses?"

Molly knit her brow and gave her a reproachful look. "Is that any way to speak to your aunt, missy?"

Without waiting for a reply, Molly forged on. "He's sent a proxy, according to the gentleman at the matchmaking agency. Once we've made the necessary arrangements, I will look into your journey. You'll travel by train, of course. I've recently invested in the Central Missouri Railroad. I can speak to someone at the office about your accommodations. Leave that to me, otherwise Mr. Anderson might have you traveling in third class."

A shiver of apprehension washed over Susanna. Molly listed off details of the trip like they were inconsequential. She hardly seemed to care Susanna would have to leave everything she knew and loved. Molly had been thinking about this for some time. That much was clear. Susanna couldn't fathom *any* part of this enterprise. Leave Albany? Without Molly? Without *Henry*? It was unthinkable.

Molly droned on. "...That should all take a few weeks or so. And will give Henry time to gather your belongings and pack them. You'll stay here with me, of course. Once you are in Texas and settled with Mr. Hopefully-Near-Death-Anderson, you can send for Henry."

Molly's eyes shone with delight. "Won't he adore Texas? Did you know he has a secret love of western novels? Don't tell him I said so. He's very bashful about his cowboy stories."

Susanna wondered how Molly could know this about Henry. She decided to ignore the comment, instead addressing Molly's grand plan. "I'm not going anywhere. I'm staying here. Near you. Henry and you are the only people I care about in the world."

Molly sighed but at least she didn't interrupt.

Undeterred, Susanna went on. "Henry's getting more stooped with each passing winter. His knees ache. His gout flares up more often. I can't stand to see him working so hard at his age. I'll buy a house, perhaps right in this neighborhood. One with a lovely porch for him to enjoy while he reads his cowboy stories."

"That's very noble. But your father would never allow such a thing. Surely you realize he'd fight you every step of the way. If you wish to escape your father, you'll need to leave Albany."

"Once I have my money, he won't have power over me."

Molly closed her eyes and for a long moment said nothing. She rose from the chesterfield and wandered across the room, stopping by the parrot's cage. The bird appeared to be dozing. He sat on his perch, unmoving.

"Susanna," Molly said softly. "I'm not joking. You must make plans to leave. I'd offer you shelter in my home, but neither Henry nor I can protect you from your father. He'll double his efforts to steal you away."

"You're overwrought. And exaggerating."

Molly reddened. "I am not exaggerating! I didn't want to tell you the details, but your father never expected you to survive childhood."

Silence stretched between them. Susanna stared at her aunt. She recoiled with horror. What on earth could Molly mean?

Molly took a few steps closer. "When you were a small child and suffered with asthma, your situation was very grim. *Very* grim. The doctors told your father on several occasions that you wouldn't live to adulthood."

Susanna's hand trembled. She'd forgotten about her cup and the tea sloshed over the rim. She set it in the saucer to keep from spilling more.

"You might not remember any of this," Molly said.

A flush of anger warmed Susanna's face. "I know how sick I was when I was a child. How could I forget struggling to breathe? Henry spent many a long night, sitting in my room, or pacing the hall, praying for each breath I managed to take. He says that his hair turned gray the first winter and he began to go bald the next." Susanna quieted. "Poor Henry."

Molly pursed her lips with dismay. Susanna knew that Molly wished it had been her at Susanna's sickbed. Molly would have toiled night and day to care for her too, but Susanna's father would never have allowed her to tend to Susanna.

"I'm sorry to bring this up," Molly said quietly.

"You need not remind me of my childhood to make a point."

"But I must make this point! I've learned more about your father's actions, sweet Susanna. I did my own investigation. I learned that your father appealed to the holding agency some time back." Molly paused before going on. "Your father demanded that the custodians of the account release the funds."

Susanna listened, wishing Molly would stop, to no avail. "It's not possible."

"When you were still just a small child," Molly said. "Your father presented letters from the doctors. The doctors wrote that it was unlikely you would live very long." Molly's voice wavered on the final words. Her eyes grew wide. Her chin trembled.

Susanna's blood chilled. Molly might be many things, but she was no liar. Susanna's heart thudded as she held her breath and waited for Molly to finish.

"There is no money," Molly said softly.

"No... money?"

Molly's eyes shone with tears that threatened to spill. "There hasn't been any money in your account for a very long time. Years. Your inheritance is gone. All of it. Your father stole every last penny."

Chapter Four

Oscar Novak (Mr. Anderson's neighbor)

At fourteen, Oscar Novak yearned for the company of men, men he could look up to. He'd never known his father, and most of his young life had been in the presence of two overbearing women, his mother and grandmother. His elderly neighbor, Mr. Anderson, was often bad-tempered, but he was successful, and honest, and Oscar respected him. And Mr. Anderson seemed to respect Oscar.

Mr. Anderson had not been well of late, and today was no exception. Mr. Anderson was laid up in bed and looked terrible. Things still needed doing, however, and there was no one except Oscar to do them. So, he began to ready the wagon to go to town, to visit the mercantile and order supplies.

Even though he knew what the answer would be, he asked his grandmother, who he called Babka, if he could make the trip by himself. The answer was no, of course. Babka explained to him, in near-perfect English, that men sometimes try to take advantage of children, and that she would not tolerate him going into town by himself at such a young age, for she and his mother would do nothing but worry about him the whole time, and would likely shorten their lives considerably if they must endure such worry, and then he would end up an orphan with no parents, and one sickly neighbor as his only friend in the world. His mama said nothing, but stared at him during the entire speech, eyes locked on his, nodding her agreement.

He had no response, which he'd learned, finally, at the age of fourteen, was always the right response. There was no arguing with either Babka or Mama. And so, he resumed getting the wagon ready and then waited for the two women to join him. Two hours later, they were standing at the counter of the mercantile.

The shopkeeper, Mr. Weber, was busy helping an elderly German woman at the other end of the counter. The woman fussed at the shopkeeper in her native language. Her words sounded harsh. Biting. But that was German for you. Babka said it was because Germans liked to grumble. Everything sounded like a complaint.

Mr. Weber kept looking over his shoulder at Oscar and his Mama, especially at Mama. Oscar didn't appreciate the way Mr. Weber seemed to look more at his Mama than at him. Finally, the elderly German woman said a few parting words and left.

"He's coming," Mama said quietly. "Do you have the list?"

"I do," Oscar replied.

Mama averted her eyes and smoothed her dark dress. Even though her English was very good, she only spoke Czech around strangers. This was true for Babka too. Both women were proud and didn't like to feel foolish, saying the wrong word or not knowing the right word in English. It was their family secret, a charade. Oscar didn't mind. He translated for both Mama and Babka, which meant he knew every detail of every conversation they had.

Mr. Weber's eyes were always a little too bright, especially when he looked at Mama. Didn't the man know better than to admire a woman who was in mourning? As he hurried down the counter, Mr. Weber failed to notice an overhead drawer had been left open, and he banged his head severely.

"Ouch!" He grabbed his head.

Serves you right.

Mama drew a sharp breath in sympathy. Mr. Weber waved away her pity. A red spot took shape on his pale forehead, accentuating the man's receding hairline.

"Hello, Oscar," he said, rubbing his head and keeping his gaze on Mama. "Mrs. Novak, very nice to see you, ma'am."

Mama smiled and nodded, dropping her gaze to her hands. She twisted her wedding ring nervously. She'd been a widow for fourteen years. Still, whenever she went to town, she wore the ring Oscar's father had given her when they'd married in Czechoslovakia. She also wore a dark dress of mourning. She was a respectable widow, and Oscar was very proud of her.

Babka wandered somewhere in the shop, also in a dark dress. She'd lost her husband years ago as well. Mourning, she explained, was a sign you loved and missed the departed.

It was a sign that the shopkeeper ignored. Clearly.

Mr. Weber stared at Mama, a foolish grin on his face.

Oscar fumed. This was not a problem when he shopped with Mr. Anderson. Oscar set the shopping list on the counter and slid it towards Mr. Weber, who made no move to take it from him.

"Mr. Anderson said to charge the farm supplies to his account," Oscar said. "The other items go on the Novak account."

"Of course." Mr. Weber called a young man over and handed him the list. Finally, Mr. Weber looked at Oscar. "How is Mr. Anderson?"

"Perfectly fine," Oscar said.

Another charade. Mr. Anderson was not well. If he'd been well, Oscar would be in town with him, not the women. He'd be speaking English only. No Czech. And he'd be spending time in the company of a wise and kind man.

Oscar was devoted to his mother and grandmother, but time with Mr. Anderson felt easier somehow. The man took time to explain things to him in a way the women never could.

The boy pushed aside his frustration. Maybe next time.

The shop clerk scurried back and forth behind the counter, gathering the items from the Novak's list and setting them in a crate. Babka watched intently from the other side of the counter. Victoria Novak, his Babka, missed nothing. She was nobody's fool.

The clerk picked a coffee can that wasn't to Babka's liking. She said no in Czech, and pointed to the crooked label and gestured for him to find a better can. A can with a straight label. When he brought a bag of salt, she made him bring all the prepacked bags. All twelve. She weighed each on a nearby scale and selected the heaviest.

Mr. Weber cleared his throat, still wearing his too-wide smile as he stared at Oscar's mother. "It's always nice to see you."

"Thank you," Oscar said, unable to resist a cheeky reply. "It's nice to see you."

Mama frowned at him. She pursed her lips with disapproval.

Mr. Weber didn't seem to notice. He set a spool of blue ribbon on the counter and spoke in a low tone. "I wonder if you might accept a little ribbon for your hair, Mrs. Novak."

Oscar recoiled. Had he missed something? The man had barely said hello and now he was presenting gifts? Mama shook her head. She blushed and looked down. Mr. Weber had a lot of nerve, pushing a present on a grieving widow! Pushy Germans.

"It's a gift," Mr. Weber said. "I saw you looking at the ribbon the other day. I don't know very much about what ladies like. Just the same, I thought the color would look pretty in your hair. You know, Mrs. Novak, I always think your hair looks like maple syrup."

Maple syrup? Oscar rolled his eyes.

His mother smiled.

"My mother doesn't like ribbons," Oscar said.

Mr. Weber set his hand over his heart and gave Mama a look with wide eyes. She laughed softly. Oscar reached across the counter, intending to push the ribbon away. Before he could reject the man's gift, his mother snatched it.

"Tank you," she said softly.

Oscar resisted a word of reproach. He'd been raised to respect his elders and knew it wasn't fitting for a boy to fuss at his mother. And maybe it wasn't right for a boy to tell a grown man his gift wasn't welcome.

That was the trouble with being the man of the house at the age of fourteen. You were in charge, until a woman said otherwise. This sort of thing was never a problem when he came to town with Mr. Anderson.

"Does old Mr. Anderson have you picking peaches?" Mr. Weber asked, turning his attention to Oscar with a cheerful smile.

"Peaches don't get ripe in September. And he's not old, sir."

"Are you going to take over the ranch when the time comes?" Mr. Weber asked.

Another blunt question. Amongst his family and people, such a direct and bold question would be considered rude. To ask about a man's affairs... that was just wrong.

"Mr. Anderson is going to be running the ranch for a long time yet."

"And what do you intend to do when you finish school next year?"

Before Oscar could answer, Babka called over her shoulder. *"Doctor!"*

Mr. Weber's brows lifted. He regarded Oscar with clear approval.

His mother beamed and wrapped her arm around his shoulders.

Oscar nodded. "One day."

"Maybe you'll open an office here in Sweet Willow," Mr. Weber said.

"Yes." The response came from his grandmother. Babka must have forgotten she didn't speak English.

Oscar let out an impatient huff. This was the third time he'd come to Sweet Willow with his Mama and Babka, and each time Mr. Weber acted more friendly. More forward. The last time they'd come to shop, he'd hinted at paying Mr. Anderson a visit.

"We must go, Mr. Weber," Oscar said, trying to keep a polite tone. "Is the order almost complete?"

"I'll see to it," the shopkeeper said. He gave Oscar's mother a final, admiring look before hurrying away to speak to his assistant.

Fortunately, things didn't take long. Soon the Novak family was ready to return home. Oscar helped the clerk load the crates in the back of the buckboard. Babka stood between the two mules, giving each animal a sugar lump as was her custom. She liked to tell them they were good souls and to thank them for their kindness.

The clerk, a young man Oscar recognized from school, glanced a few times at Babka as she spoke to the mules. He grinned at Oscar, who responded with a shrug and slight smile. Oscar was used to curious glances from strangers who weren't from Czech families. The Novaks were different and proud of it.

Mr. Weber came to the front of the store, a dog following on his heels. Oscar's breath caught. What a dog. The sun shone on the dog's coat. She was a hound dog, the best kind of dog as far as he was concerned. Copper, the color of a new penny. She lay down and closed her eyes to doze in the sun.

Oscar moved without thinking, drawing closer.

"I heard that about you," said Mr. Weber.

The words startled Oscar. Mr. Weber regarded him with a lopsided smile.

"Sir?"

"One of the boys in the stock room said you love dogs. That you've befriended a few mongrels around the school. They say dogs take to you."

Oscar shoved his hands into his pockets. "Dogs are okay."

"Sadie had pups last week. They're wearing her out. She likes to come outside every so often to get away, I suppose."

"How many did she have?"

"Six."

"What will you do with them?"

"Sell them. I have two spoken for already. The sire is the best dog I've ever known. Sadie here is smart as a whip."

Sadie opened her eyes and thumped her tail. She lifted her head and fixed her gaze on Oscar. Some dogs had a way about them, something in their eyes that showed how intelligent they were. Oscar might not like Mr. Weber much, but he liked the man's expression. Sadie was definitely smart. Smart as a whip.

"Next time you come, I'll show you her pups, if you like."

Oscar wasn't sure what to say. If he came with his mother and grandmother, seeing the pups would be impossible.

Mr. Weber spoke again. "You're a good son to your mother. A good grandson to Mrs. Novak. You take good care of your family, don't you?"

Oscar would like to think the man's words were true. He remained silent, however, uncertain how to respond.

"Oscar!" Babka's voice made him retreat a few steps.

"Thank you, sir," Oscar said quietly.

Mr. Weber nodded and winked.

Oscar helped Mama and Babka to the buckboard, and soon they were on their way home. They drove in silence. The quiet gave him a chance to think about the dog.

Sadie. All dogs were good, but hounds were special. Sturdy. Hard-working. Loyal.

He winced as he thought about Sadie's puppies. Picturing a half-dozen small puppies like Sadie made something hurt inside his chest. Mr. Anderson didn't have a dog. He said he'd owned many over the years, but when the last one died, he didn't have the heart for a new one.

Everyone had different opinions about dogs. Mama didn't understand them and preferred cats. Babka had terrible scars down her arm from getting bitten as a child. And Mr. Anderson missed his old dogs so much he got teary-eyed just thinking about them.

When the Novaks had come to Sweet Willow five months ago, Oscar had dared to hope for a dog. For the first time, his family had their own home. They had room for Babka's enormous garden. A place for Mama's flowers. But no dog for

Oscar. It was not to be. Mr. Anderson said no, as did Babka. So, the matter was settled.

Chapter Five

Beau

The outpost lay on the outskirts of Houston. It was run by a Ranger who wasn't too pleased to see Beau Bailey riding up. Captain Maddox didn't appreciate getting orders about taking on a man he didn't personally select. Not only that, he had a man on the job and saw no reason to let Beau take his place.

He met Beau in front of the outpost, a scowl etched on his face.

"What makes you think you can do better?" the captain said, not bothering with preliminaries.

"I don't know why I think I can do better, but I usually manage all right," Beau replied.

"I'll tell you right now, I don't like getting a new man. Not one bit."

Beau was tired and hungry. All he wanted was to check into a hotel, one with a bed and bath and hot meal would be swell too. He was a little taken aback by Maddox's tone. Usually, his superiors treated him with respect. He was no greenhorn. No fresh recruit.

The introduction was a little abrupt, even for a man with the reputation of Captain Maddox. The man probably should have hung up his spurs a few years back. He'd outlived his glory days. Maddox had tracked down a murderer in Kerr

County twenty years ago. It had been a tough case that ended in a shootout.

Maddox managed to collar the killer even though he'd been shot. Twice. He'd received the fame he craved but it cost him. The wounds festered and he'd lost his right arm. The tough Ranger stayed in the service but made sure everyone knew about his heroics.

"Is there some reason you didn't want to stay with your own outfit in El Paso?" Maddox demanded.

"I've got a warm spot in my heart for Houston," Beau drawled.

"You're not going to end up with another story splashed across the paper, Bailey."

Maddox turned to spit, just to make his displeasure perfectly clear. He turned on his heel and trudged up the steps to his office.

Beau followed. Once more, he regretted the story in the newspaper. He'd imagined that the article had run in Fort Worth and only there. Now he wondered if it had been picked up and run in other papers.

"I reckon I'm stuck with you." The captain crossed the cramped office, stopping in front of a large map hanging on the wall. "But I'm not happy to switch horses midstream. Are you sure you didn't stir up trouble in El Paso?"

"No, sir. No trouble at all." He didn't bother telling Maddox about the number of men he'd arrested in El Paso. He eyed the map of Texas and tried to offer a lighthearted comment in hopes of changing the captain's surly demeanor. "I like to move around. It suits me to see different parts of the great state of Texas."

"I prefer Rangers stay put."

The captain eyed him with clear disdain. Beau could tell that the man didn't just dislike new men, but him in particular. He didn't care. Not much. His work would be on a train, not with Captain Maddox. Working alone always suited him best.

"Once I find the Craddick men, I'll move on. How's that?"

"I don't have any say in the matter."

"Is there some reason you don't want a new man on the job? You've had three months to bring them in."

The captain curled his lip. His eyes flashed with anger. He wasn't used to being challenged. Beau wasn't either, and while he didn't like to tangle with a superior, he wasn't about to back down. Not when innocent lives were at stake.

"We almost had them." The captain's tone was pure contempt. "*Twice.*"

"I heard. That's not anything to boast about. One of your men abandoned his post to play cards. Another man dallied with his sweetheart and missed the train in Lufkin."

The captain turned to face him. "You seem pretty sure of yourself, Bailey. You've got a big head."

Beau nodded. "That may be so, but I won't let the men slip through my fingers. I don't play cards. And I don't have a sweetheart."

Captain Maddox's gaze moved to Beau's scars. He sneered. "There's a surprise. With your looks, I'd think the ladies would be lining up."

"Not when I'm on the job." Beau narrowed his eyes. "Sir."

The captain turned to the map. "You'll be riding the train from Houston to Palestine and back again. The Craddick brothers have robbed three women. They favor young, pretty women who travel alone. They pick 'em out. One of them strikes up a conversation while the other does the filching."

Beau hadn't ever dealt with outlaws that targeted women. A surge of protectiveness sparked inside his chest. He curled his fingers into a fist.

The captain grunted. "You'd think a woman would have the sense not to talk to a stranger."

"You make it sound like the women bring it on themselves."

"Darned right. I don't see why I need to send my best men to mind a bunch of womenfolk who can't keep their mouths shut."

Beau gritted his teeth and turned away. He crossed the office, stopping at the door. "A woman deserves safe passage on a train as much as the next person. I'll be at the depot first thing in the morning."

The captain said nothing. He shrugged and kept his attention on the map. Maddox was exactly the type of man who gave the Texas Rangers a bad name. The captain likely didn't see the value in bringing in a pair of criminals that hadn't made a big name for themselves. Where was the glory in arresting men who preyed on women? Especially women who ought to know better.

Beau prided himself on controlling his temper, but he felt the distinct spark of anger. He resolved to leave the captain's office. Immediately. Before he said something that he regretted.

Chapter Six

Oscar

It took half the ride home, but Oscar finally pushed aside thoughts of Sadie and her puppies. It didn't do any good to imagine something you couldn't have. Instead, he thought of the chores that waited for him. Almost at once his mind went to concerns about Mr. Anderson who had still been in bed when they left.

He urged the mules a little faster, but the animals, being even more stubborn than most mules, plodded at their own pace. The trip home gave Oscar plenty of time to imagine the worst – Mr. Anderson waking and calling for help, and no one there to help; Mr. Anderson feeling worse than usual; Mr. Anderson stumbling as he had last week and hitting his chin on the dresser.

Finally, the homestead came into view. To his relief, Mr. Anderson sat on the porch, rocking in his chair.

Oscar unhitched the team and tended to the animals. He hurried to Mr. Anderson's home. The path led past the cabin of Mr. Anderson's late brother, William, who had died earlier in the year, before the Novaks had come to Sweet Willow.

The cabin looked empty. Sad. Babka said houses didn't like being empty.

"I'm about to die of starvation," Mr. Anderson shouted from his porch. "If your grandma tries to feed me more of that garlic soup, I'm not eating."

Oscar suppressed a grin. Mr. Anderson was hungry. Good. Oscar wanted to point out that last night's garlic soup had clearly restored the man's strength. But Robert Anderson would have only scoffed. And grumbled.

"No garlic soup, sir. She's making *kulajda.*"

Mr. Anderson knit his brow. "With potatoes?"

"Yes, sir."

Oscar ascended the steps to the porch. He passed Will Anderson's rocker, making certain to give it a wide berth. Anytime someone got near his brother's chair, Mr. Anderson fretted they might sit down, a notion which troubled the old man greatly.

Instead, Oscar crossed the porch and went to the corner by the geraniums. From this spot he could enjoy the view of the pastures and orchard, a sight which always filled his heart with a soft comfort. He could tell that Mr. Anderson felt better and might even want to "talk a spell."

"What you got planned?" Mr. Anderson asked.

From the beginning, Mr. Anderson had started conversations about work chores with this question. He always wanted to know what Oscar had in mind. This was so different from his mother and grandmother who always wanted to make clear what *they* had in mind.

Mr. Anderson regarded him with respect and treated him like he was already a man.

"I will fix the gate on the south pasture. Tend to the animals and haul water to my grandmother's garden. After that, I will grease the buckboard's axle and mend the harness. This evening I must work on my lessons."

"I'd like to see the donkeys. Do you have time to bring the boys up from the pasture?"

"I always have time to bring the boys to see you."

Mr. Anderson didn't pay much attention to most of the animals on the ranch, but the trio of donkeys held a special place in his heart. After his brother died, he'd come across the three animals abandoned in a field. He figured they'd come from the Sierra Mines. The donkeys were nothing but skin and bones.

Mr. Anderson admitted to Oscar that he'd missed his brother something terrible. The little donkeys made him feel a little less lonesome. He'd doted on the animals as if they were his children. In no time, they'd gotten fat and sassy.

Oscar's mother loved the donkeys too. She'd named them after angels. Mr. Anderson said he thought the names suited the little donkeys. He always brightened when Oscar brought them by the cabin. The simple request pleased Oscar immensely. If Mr. Anderson was asking about the donkeys, he might be feeling stronger.

"I'll bring the donkeys." Oscar folded his arms across his chest. "After you've eaten your supper. My grandmother will bring it soon."

Mr. Anderson leaned forward in his chair and rapped his cane on the wood floor. He knit his brow, but his eyes held a spark of amusement. "I need to tell you something."

"Yes, sir."

Often Mr. Anderson's words, "I need to tell you something," led to stories from his youth, opinions about sundry topics or instructions about his passing. *Take good care of the donkeys. Don't let my no-good nephew step foot on my ranch. After I'm gone, bury me beside Will. Don't let the dang rooster roam the barnyard.*

Today seemed different, however. The man looked bright-eyed. Oscar hoped there would be no more talk of what to do after he passed.

Mr. Anderson gave him a pointed look. "Your grandma scares me."

Oscar suppressed a smile. "Yes, sir. She scares everyone."

"Ever since I got to feeling poorly, she's been coming over here, fussing over me, making me eat garlic soup, garlic noodles, garlic dumplings. She's even *smiling*!"

They shared a laugh and lapsed into an amiable quiet.

Ever since the Novaks had come to the ranch, his grandmother and Mr. Anderson squabbled. The Novaks had come to work for Mr. Anderson in return for lodging and a small wage. The arrangement had suited everyone until he'd offered to give them property.

Babka had been rendered speechless. When she recovered her senses, she explained, firmly, that the Novaks didn't take charity. Even when Mr. Anderson told her he wanted to give them the land to keep it away from his greedy, no-good nephew, she refused. She'd held Oscar up as part of the reason. Novak men didn't till the soil. They became doctors.

In the end, they compromised. Mr. Anderson convinced her to accept the cabin and garden, a small parcel of land on the corner of the Anderson ranch. Babka insisted on paying what she could, giving him most of the family's meager savings.

Mr. Anderson complained about the Novak ladies, calling them impossible and cantankerous. And the Novak ladies said the same about Mr. Anderson.

Mr. Anderson rocked in his chair. "Your grandma smiles at me nowadays. It gets me thinking I must be on my way to meet the good Lord. Terrifying woman. Your mamma won't ever find a good man if the poor fella has to contend with Victoria Novak."

"Yes, sir." Oscar wouldn't argue.

Mr. Anderson raised his cane and pointed it up the path towards the orchard. "I coulda left all this to your grandma if she hadn't been so obstinate. Now I gotta send off for a bride. Else my no-good nephew will waltz onto my ranch and lay claim."

"I'm sorry, sir." His voice caught in his throat. Oscar wished his mother and grandmother weren't so set in their ways. He would have gladly taken the ranch. He scanned the vast fields, the groves of trees and the peach orchard. If he owned a ranch, he'd get a hound dog. No, he'd get a *dozen* hound dogs.

Mr. Anderson had threatened to get married before, but nothing had come of it. His ideas were just that – ideas.

A month after they came to Sweet Willow, he fell ill with a fever. He stumbled down the path to the Novak cabin to offer a marriage in name only to Oscar's grandmother. Or mother. He didn't much care who became Mrs. Anderson, just so long as Jack Anderson didn't get his greedy, grimy hands on the property.

Babka and Mama had hurried him back home and tucked him into his bed. They never spoke of the man's marriage proposal, pretending it had never happened.

Mr. Anderson thought of property in the same way some men thought of money. He figured people ought to want as much of it as they could get.

He never understood how any woman who had buried a husband was honor-bound to grieve. She must dress in dark, somber dress until the day she joined her beloved. To marry again would bring dishonor to the memory of their late husbands. Ridiculous.

Novaks didn't accept charity.

Novaks didn't farm the land and they most definitely didn't marry twice.

The wind stirred, moving across the pasture like a rustling wave. Oscar tried to push his worries aside. Mr. Anderson would be fine. Everything would be fine.

"Hallo, Robert!" His grandmother's voice rang out.

Mr. Anderson yelped. "Mercy. Here she comes. Smiling again."

Babka headed up the path, holding a cast iron pot with a quilted oven mitt. "I am so pleased to see you sitting in your rocker chair."

"Lord, help me," Mr. Anderson muttered.

"I made soup!" She hefted the pot to make her point.

"Soup. It's always soup." Mr. Anderson frowned at Oscar. "What is it with your people and soup?"

"Soup makes you strong," Babka said. "It's good when you're sick, but it's good when you're well too. Eat soup each day, and you'll live a long life."

"Bah. Do you actually live any longer? Or does it just *seem* that way?"

As Babka drew near, the fragrant aroma of the soup wafted through the air. Oscar opened the door to the cabin for his grandmother.

She paused at the top of the steps and smiled happily at Mr. Anderson. "Elsa will bring a plate. She made rizek. You like this, Robert. Yes?"

"Don't know what you're talkin' about."

"She make a few weeks ago. It's...eh...meat."

"That don't tell me much."

Oscar made a move to take the heavy pot from his grandmother, but she shooed him.

"It's meat from the cows. You know?"

"Beef?"

"Yes!"

He shrugged.

Babka tried a different tact. "It's like schnitzel." She said the word with derision.

"Well, there's something I understand." He heaved himself out of the chair. "I've had schnitzel a time or two. Germans like to serve schnitzel at weddings around these parts. 'Course they wash it down with a little beer. Those Germans know how to throw a good party."

Babka's lips thinned. "My people have better parties. More fun."

"Sure, they do. Why, anyone with two working eyes can see how much fun you are, Victoria." Mr. Anderson winked at Oscar. "Always dressed in black. Plain to see that you're just a barrel of laughs."

His grandmother knit her brow. She didn't always grasp what Mr. Anderson said, but she nodded like she understood and carried the soup inside. After she set the pot down, she busied herself with setting the table for Mr. Anderson. She fussed under her breath, complaining in Czech about the old man's untidy home.

Mr. Anderson limped across the porch, leaning heavily on his cane. A few paces from Oscar, he paused and swayed on his feet. A sheen of sweat shone on his forehead. Oscar moved quickly. He darted to the man's side and took hold of his arm.

"I'm fine, dang it," Mr. Anderson growled. "Just fine."

"Yes, sir," Oscar said quietly.

The man leaned heavily against Oscar's shoulder. For a moment, neither spoke. Mr. Anderson's ragged breath seemed to take all his strength. He groaned as he drew himself straight.

Each night, Oscar prayed to God. He prayed for Mr. Anderson's strength and health and he prayed for more time with the old-timer. He'd never had a father, or a grandfather and Mr. Anderson seemed to be a little of both. The man knew so much about the land. Oscar was learning, but he still had a long way to go.

Despite Oscar's hopes and prayers, Mr. Anderson had grown weaker. Oscar noted the man's diminished size. He'd lost weight. Just a few short months ago, he'd been tireless. Strong and robust. But now he seemed frail.

"All right, son. Give me a hand to the table," Mr. Anderson said.

Oscar helped him inside, taking him to the table where Babka ladled the steaming soup into a bowl. Mr. Anderson gave Oscar a weary smile and winked.

Babka chattered about the weather as she sliced a fresh loaf of bread. In a lively tone, she spoke of the fine, clear day. It was as pretty as a picture. Anyone could see that. But her wrists troubled her that morning. And that always happened when the weather was due to change. It was a sign, she said with conviction. A sign she could feel in the very marrow of her bones.

"Mark my words," she said cheerfully. "A storm is coming."

Chapter Seven

Susanna

Two days after Susanna came to the home of Aunt Molly, Henry arrived to visit. He was terribly worried about her after the argument in the Astor home. Susanna tried to ease his fears. She didn't mention the inheritance. Neither did Henry, making her wonder if he already knew. Instead, she turned her attention to Molly's plans for her.

They spoke in Molly's sitting room. Henry paced back and forth. Susanna could see that Molly's idea made him even more fretful.

"It's a marriage in name only," she explained. "Molly's certain that if I remain in Albany, I'll never have any peace from my father."

"I can't begin to imagine you getting on a train and leaving. It's not possible. I won't be party to one of Molly's schemes."

Susanna drew a sharp breath. She was grateful her aunt had not yet come downstairs. Molly would have taken offense at Henry's choice of words.

"I'm certain your aunt is exaggerating," Henry continued with growing frustration. "Your father is strong-willed, but he's still your father. He'll see the error of his ways. Eventually."

"More than anything, my father likes to win. His marriage to my mother soured and he wants to punish me. He said as much the other night. Every time he looks at me, he sees her."

"Men like your father say all manner of things in the heat of the moment."

"It's as if you're defending him. My father!"

"I am. It's true. Not because I hold him in high regard. It's because I can't imagine..." His words trailed off. He stopped by the fireplace, bowed his head, and leaned against the mantle.

Susanna's heart skipped a beat. She stared with growing alarm. Henry had always been her rock. Suddenly he looked old, tired, defeated. Her heart squeezed with pain. She recalled Molly's comment about his western novels. The urge to change the subject came over her. She snatched Mr. Anderson's letter from the end table and began to relay the contents.

"He's lost his brother and is tired of being alone. He wants nothing more than a companion. Someone to inherit his land and in return care for his animals. Especially his donkeys."

Henry stared with an expression of stunned disbelief. "Donkeys?"

"Wait, Henry. Listen to what he wrote. It's really so charming." Before he could object, she read the part of the letter that had stirred her heart.

Just ornery donkeys that do nothing all day but eat and doze under the oak trees. They're cranky, just like me, I suppose. Folks might think I'm crazy, but I care for them. At the end of a long day, it warms my heart to see them. They come when I call. They want nothing more than a scratch between their ears and a little feed. In my old age, I've taken to them. I hope you do too, and after I'm gone, I'd like to think you'd dote on them like I do. I've always thought animals were better than most folks. They say that the good Lord blessed donkeys and that's why they have a cross on their back. My no-good nephew, Jack, seems to think I'll leave the land to him since he's my only kin. I won't leave a dime to that worthless so and so. Not if I have a kind-hearted wife who'd care for my donkeys.

She set the letter aside, expecting to find Henry a little less pale and shaken, but he still looked dumbfounded. Perhaps more so.

"Mr. Anderson sent a ledger filled with notes about his property and animals. He writes so tenderly of his family's home, the orchards and all the different creatures that he cares for, I feel as though I already know him. Especially the donkeys."

The moment she finished, she realized how absurd it must sound.

He gestured to one of the birdcages. A pair of finches hopped around, peeping cheerfully. "Molly's affection for collecting animals must be catching. You spend a few days in her home and now you want to raise a pair of donkeys."

Susanna lifted her chin. "I won't be insulted. And there are three of them, not two."

Henry ran his hand over his balding head. He gestured to the windows facing the garden. "Maybe you can get a flock of flamingos."

"You're not amusing."

Susanna folded her hands. He was, perhaps, a little amusing, but she wouldn't give him the satisfaction of telling him. She was relieved that he seemed less distraught, however.

"I told your father I would try to bring you home."

"I won't go. I told him I intended to stay with Aunt Molly until I married Mr. Wiggins. That will give me time to make my own plans. I sent him a note this morning."

Henry let out an exasperated huff. His stoic demeanor rarely gave way, but he was most definitely showing signs of deep concern. At least, he wasn't as distressed as a few moments ago. Or as pale and shaken.

He returned to pacing the room, hands clasped behind his back. "I will put some thought into a plan for you. Something sensible. I have a little money tucked away, money I always intended to leave to you."

"Henry, I do appreciate your-"

He stopped her with a raised hand. "I don't like to speak ill of people, but your Aunt Molly is unhinged."

Susanna was about to argue vigorously, but Dimitri, the parrot, interrupted with a loud squawk.

"Molly is unhinged. Molly is unhinged."

"My word," Susanna marveled as she rose to her feet. "Dimitri has never spoken before."

"Oh, dear," Henry said, looking horror-struck. "Oh, dear me."

They went to the cage.

Dimitri studied Henry with interest, tilting his head. *"Molly is unhinged."*

"You're a very naughty bird," Henry chided. He turned to Susanna. "Molly will know that I said that. No doubt in my mind. She'll never forgive me."

"Never forgive me."

Susanna shook her head. "Not at all. She'll be delighted he's finally talking. She's trying to teach him to say, 'Hubert is a thief.'"

"What's that supposed to mean?"

56

Susanna reproached herself for mentioning the word "thief" to Henry. He might not know about the inheritance and she didn't want to add to his list of worries. "It's nothing. Nothing at all."

"You are a poor liar. You always have been, even as a small child. Your mother was just the same. Completely lacking in guile."

Susanna resented the remark but could hardly argue. Henry knew her too well.

There was a shout on the street. Henry went to the window. The next sound came from the front door. Banging. Clamor. More shouting.

Susanna peered out the door of the sitting room.

A servant opened the door. A trio of thickly muscled men filled the doorway. The servant screamed, pushed the door and ran down the hall. One of the men jammed his foot in the door, keeping it open. The cook, a stout older woman, appeared. She stepped in front of him, preventing the men from barging into the home.

Susanna listened as the men demanded Mr. Astor's daughter.

"We was told to use force if necessary," the group's leader snarled.

The cook lifted a rolling pin over her head. The men scrambled back. The cook slammed the door shut. The men shouted and banged on the door.

Henry crossed the room, a look of indignation on his face. "This is most unseemly. I shall put an end to this rude display. What can this be about?"

Susanna stopped him, grabbing his sleeve. "Stay here," she hissed. "I've seen them before. They work for my father. They'll leave soon enough."

"Those men will break down the door. I intend to speak to them and send them on their way."

"Henry, you will *not* speak to those rough men."

A movement caught their attention. Molly descended the stairs. Calm, cool and utterly composed, Molly swept down the wide stairs, clad in an elegant gown. Her hair was artfully arranged. Her jewels sparkled in the morning light.

Henry drew a sharp breath. He was, thankfully, too surprised to speak.

Molly hummed as she crossed the foyer to the front door. When she flung the door open, she found the men standing on her threshold. They recoiled, confused looks on all three faces. None had expected the lady of the house to greet them. The group retreated a few steps.

Susanna scurried to the window to watch without danger of being seen by the men. Henry followed. She opened the window a notch.

Molly stood on her threshold and addressed the startled men with a voice that rang across the quiet, tree-lined street. She waved a newspaper in the air like a queen with her scepter.

"You *dare* come for my niece in the days before her wedding?" Using the newspaper, she smacked the nearest man on his head. "You think the poor girl can manage a wedding on her own?"

Molly was like an avenging angel, bent on punishing the men for daring to set one disreputable boot on her front step.

The men were so surprised, they could do nothing more than stare at Molly as she heaped insults on their heads. Molly was in rare form. Even Susanna was stunned.

Residents of the well-to-do neighborhood stopped to watch. Pedestrians paused. Neighbors opened their doors and looked up and down the street to find the source of the commotion.

"What do you intend?" she shouted. "To take *Susanna Astor* back to the home of her father, *Hubert Astor*?"

The men glanced back and forth in bewilderment. Molly used their confusion to her advantage. She managed two more well-placed blows with her newspaper. The men held up their hands to ward off any more abuse.

Molly went on. "You tell Mr. Astor that Susanna will remain with me. Unless he wishes to manage the details of the wedding himself. Why the poor girl doesn't even have a *wedding frock*!"

A wave of indignation moved over the growing crowd. A milkman set down his delivery and shook his fist. A lady stood in the doorway of the house across the street, shoulder to shoulder with a scullery maid. They turned to each other with dismay.

"Susanna's mother passed when she was only a child," Molly proclaimed. "She's practically an *orphan*."

More indignation.

Susanna guessed this wasn't the first time Molly had created a scene. Her neighbors were likely used to commotions playing out at Molly's door. A few children appeared from a home next door. When they spied Molly standing in her doorway, they immediately sat on the top step to watch and listen.

Molly rained more abuse upon the men. She paused for effect too, allowing her words to hang in the air. With each passing moment, the men shrank lower and inched away. Susanna expected them to bolt down the street. The crowd began booing and shouting insults.

Molly flung the paper at the men. "Hubert didn't even bother to make the announcement. I've done so on the poor girl's behalf. He can read it for himself on *page seventeen*."

Across the street, a neighbor pulled his newspaper from under his arm and quickly popped it open. He began leafing through the pages. Others crowded around him, eager to catch a glimpse of Molly's announcement.

Susanna hadn't realized Molly had published a wedding notice, but she shouldn't have been surprised. Her aunt told her over dinner the night before that the only way Susanna might escape her father's plot to marry her off was to pretend to comply.

"If I see you again," Molly shouted, "I shall call the constable."

Voices rang out from several houses. *Here, here. You heard her boys. Be gone. Scoundrels! The poor, motherless girl!*

With that, the men fled. They ran down the street in a panic. Onlookers jeered.

Henry didn't move. He remained staring at the spot where the men had stood. After a long moment, he rubbed his forehead and spoke. "I never imagined your father would stoop so low."

"You see why I can't return?"

"I do. And I must admit, Molly has likely stopped any more notions your father might have about forcing you to come home."

Susanna agreed. "It was a very good deception. I must say."

Henry muttered under his breath, offering words of grudging admiration. He added, "I take back what I said about your aunt."

Molly, in that precise moment, swept into the room. "What did you say about me?"

Susanna couldn't resist glancing at Dimitri, half-expecting the bird to betray Henry, but he dozed on his perch.

Henry tugged his sleeves and clasped his hands behind his back. "I didn't agree with your plan to send Susanna to Texas. At first."

Molly pouted. "But now you see that it's brilliant. And that I am, in fact, brilliant?"

Henry considered his response, looking displeased, until finally he reluctantly replied, "Yes. All that."

Chapter Eight

Susanna

The next few days passed in a whir of activity. It was as if Aunt Molly worried that if Susanna had a moment or two of peace, she'd change her mind. Molly had trunks delivered from a luggage shop in town. She and Susanna packed clothing and shoes and personal belongings.

Henry managed to bring many of her possessions without anyone in the Astor home noticing. Together, the three of them arrived at a plan to spirit Susanna to the train station. Both Molly and Henry fretted over the details. The plan involved a maid who would act as a decoy, dressing as Susanna and taking a carriage to a dress shop while Susanna went to the train station.

Susanna thought Molly and Henry worried unnecessarily. However, since they so rarely agreed on anything, she decided not to argue. On a dismal, rainy morning they set off for the Albany train station.

Henry met them on the platform. They spoke briefly, standing under umbrellas in the drizzle. She'd expected an argument from the kindly man, but he wore a weary smile. She was certain he forced himself to have a cheerful expression.

"I never imagined there would come a day I'd collaborate with Molly," he said. "I've packed two trunks of books. They've been taken to your first-class cabin."

"You won't board first class, however," Molly said. "I wouldn't put it past Hubert to post men around the station. They won't look for you in third class. Once the train leaves Albany, the porter will move you to better accommodations."

"I pray they won't search for me." Susanna set her hand over her heart. "Heavens, what if they come to... all the w-way to Texas?"

Henry shook his head. "They won't. If you are married, you won't be worth the trouble."

Susanna nodded, her worry ebbing somewhat.

"It sounds harsh," Molly said. "But Henry's right."

"You'll come visit me, won't you?" Susanna asked.

Molly nodded. "Of course."

"I don't know," Henry replied.

"He'll come," Molly said.

"I'd be in the way," Henry said, his tone morose. "You don't need me anymore."

Susanna grew flustered. "But I assumed-"

The train whistle blasted, piercing the cold morning air. The conductor called an all aboard. Molly pushed the tickets into Susanna's gloved hands and kissed her cheek. Henry drew her into an awkward embrace. Tears shone in his eyes.

The whistle blew again.

"Go," urged Molly. "Have a safe trip and write the minute you get there."

Susanna gave them a final embrace. She hurried to the door and boarded the train, behind the few final stragglers. The conductor ushered her to her seat. The train lurched and began its slow departure. Susanna watched Molly and Henry until they disappeared.

Suddenly overcome by a swell of emotions, she put her face in her hands and let out a quiet sob. She remained in her seat, hiding behind her hands as the train gathered speed. The rhythmic cadence of the wheels slowly helped her to regain her composure.

She lowered her hands and pressed her palm to the window. The landscape flew past, faster and faster. She was leaving home. Leaving everything she knew. The good, the bad and the in-between. What would she find in Texas? It was impossible to say, but one thing she knew, nothing would ever be the same.

Chapter Nine

Beau

Beau made his way down the train car, pausing at each compartment to eye the passengers. Miners and young cowboys filled the third-class car. The cowboys traveled to Houston. The miners traveled to West Texas.

The men passed bottles of spirits back and forth. They'd grown raucous and rowdy since he passed through earlier. The language was a tad rough. Later, there'd likely be a brawl or two which wasn't his concern, thankfully.

The first-class car held a more refined crowd, mostly older gentlemen traveling with their wives. Most had dined already and played cards or read. Later, many would retire to the sleeping car, but many would spend the night in less comfort, dozing in their chairs.

After two weeks riding trains, he hadn't seen the Craddick brothers. The trips back and forth had been uneventful. They'd been dull, truth be told. Tonight felt different. He couldn't put his finger on why, but he sensed a change.

He worked his way further down the last car, opening doors and checking out the passengers. Whenever he investigated the compartments, he noted the same alarmed response. He didn't intend to, but he frightened folks. Men glared. Women cried out in fright. He'd tap his badge to show he was a trusted lawman, a Texas Ranger. Usually, the badge would ease their fears, but sometimes the passengers couldn't get past the scars on his face.

Either way, the fine folks in first class always seemed relieved when he nodded, said a few polite words, and moved on.

He moved cautiously to inspect the last compartment. When he looked inside, he found only one passenger. A woman. A young woman.

He stood in the doorway and studied her with curiosity. She sat by the window, reading. With the sun sinking in the west, soft rays of sunshine lit the interior. The woman was so absorbed in her book she didn't notice him standing three steps away.

Her lack of awareness gave him the chance to admire the pretty girl. Coppery locks swept into an elegant arrangement, one that showed off her pale, creamy skin. Her narrow shoulders accentuated her feminine form. She knit her brow as she read, forming two small lines between arched brows. Her book caused some concern, judging from the way she bit the edge of her lower lip.

Transfixed, he remained in the doorway, watching with a mix of interest and bemusement.

Her perfect posture suggested she'd gone to some fancy finishing school. Her dress looked freshly pressed and spotless, unlike the other ladies on the train. They all wore rumpled dresses and looked shabby in comparison.

She continued reading as the train rumbled along the track. She was completely unaware of a stranger watching her. Good thing he wasn't one of the Craddicks. He could have robbed her three times over by now, and with all the racket, not one other passenger would have been the wiser.

A wash of irritation heated his thoughts. The girl was vulnerable, traveling alone through remote and desolate Texas timber country. This was exactly the type of victim the Craddicks preyed upon. How had any self-respecting father, brother or husband allowed such a lovely and delicate woman to set out on her own?

She was the only woman on the train traveling alone. If the Craddicks were on the train, they'd be very interested in a woman like her. Wealthy, distracted by her book, slight build, this young lady would suit their needs perfectly.

He removed his hat and shifted his gun belt back a notch so it wouldn't cause alarm. "Miss," he said quietly, hoping not to startle her.

She looked up, blinked a few times, and smiled politely. "I've already shown my ticket."

"I'm a Ranger."

She looked at him as if she didn't understand. "What's a Ranger?"

The girl didn't know about Rangers? Some folks feared the Rangers. Others admired the men who served, but he'd never met a person who didn't know what a Ranger was. Her blank look stung his pride.

"I work for the state of Texas."

Her gaze drifted from his eyes to the rest of him and all the way to his boots. A crease formed between her delicate brows. Her lips tugged downward as she tried to figure out just what he did, or what he was.

"I'm a lawman."

Her eyes lit up with surprise. "Oh, my."

He kept his gaze on her, trying to ignore the soft scent wafting in the air. "Are you stopping in Houston?"

"I am. After that, I'm traveling to a town by the name of..." her words trailed off. "I believe it's called Sweet William." She closed her book and set it down. Taking a deep breath, it seemed she was summoning her nerve to say more. "I'm a mail-order bride."

Her cheeks colored to a delicate pink. He watched as the blush bloomed across her fair skin. Rubbing the back of his neck, he grimaced and wondered what in tarnation was wrong with him. It wasn't like him to dwell on a girl's blushed cheeks.

"Do you mean Sweet Willow?"

Her color deepened. "Yes, I believe you're right. Do you know the town?"

"I do, in fact." He gestured to the seat across from her. "May I?"

"Well..." she said hesitantly. "All right."

He chose the seat that was the furthest from the girl. He wanted to point out that she was on her way to marry a stranger. She shouldn't be so choosy about a lawman sitting with her.

"It might be best if you have company as the evening wears on," he said. "I'm riding this train to provide protection."

Her eyes widened.

"You can rest assured I mean no harm," he said.

She nodded slowly as if not entirely sure if she should trust him.

The girl wore a floral fragrance. Just a hint. Not heavy like many other ladies. Annoyance jabbed at him. He wondered about the lucky man waiting for her. He knew plenty of people in Sweet Willow and wanted to ask the man's name. It wasn't good manners, though. Heck, he didn't even know *her* name. He'd been so struck by her that he'd forgotten basic manners.

"My name's Beau Bailey."

"My name is Susanna Astor. Pleased to meet you."

"Astor," he remarked with surprise. The name seemed familiar. She might be part of the moneyed crowd. Her clothes were plenty fancy, so why would she sign up to be a mail-order bride?

"I'm sorry. I need to remember I'm married now. My last name is Anderson."

Anderson? He gave a murmur of surprise. There was another familiar name. Only this one he knew a little better since it was from Sweet Willow. There were two men in Sweet Willow by the name of Anderson. Brothers. Will and Robert. Two cantankerous and very elderly bachelors.

They had more money than Solomon, but folks always said that you wouldn't know it from the looks of things around the Anderson Ranch.

The men were bad-tempered. Or so he'd heard. Of course, some people said that about him. One thing was sure, either Anderson fella was old enough to be Susanna's grandfather.

He wondered if she realized how old her husband was.

Why would either of them take a wife?

He marveled at the astonishing idea. It wasn't possible. How could this sweet young woman have married one of the Anderson brothers? His mind rebelled, refusing to accept the idea. The marriage probably came about because of the men's unending quarrels. One of the brothers probably took a wife just to spite the other.

"I'll be," he muttered.

Noting his dismay, Susanna averted her eyes and turned away to look out the window. The last rays of dusk cast a soft glow over her features. He could hardly tear his eyes from her. He forced himself to look away.

He recalled a story he'd heard about the Anderson brothers. While visiting his cousin Noah, who'd just adopted six boys and taken a wife, Noah's eldest son, Holden, told of an event at the family's auction barn.

The two Anderson brothers had become embroiled in a bidding war, against each other. Their tempers flared as usual. The argument was absurd. They lived on the same ranch. Their animals were all part of the same herd. That logic didn't slow the men down, however.

A crowd gathered to see who would get the winning bid.

As the story reached its climax, Josiah, Noah's youngest, interrupted Holden. He stood up, knocking over his chair and finished the tale. "And then, wouldn't you know, Will Anderson keels over, dead. *Dead.* Dead I tell you. Dead as a doorknob!"

Beau smiled at the memory. The boys had snickered, covering their mouths with their hands. They didn't want to laugh at a story about a man meeting his maker. The poor man had died while trying to win a bid just for the sake of winning.

Just the same, Josiah's comment about doorknobs amused the rest of the boys.

The reference to doorknobs sparked an immediate argument. Was it dead as a doorknob, or dead as a doornail? No one could say, exactly. One of the boys suggested dead as a dodo. Even Noah had joined the lively discussion while his wife merely sighed and shook her head.

Beau thought about the evening. He was almost certain the boys had said it was Will Anderson that had died. Or was it Robert? Beau pushed the memory aside. He'd be certain to find out more the next time he traveled to Sweet Willow.

Setting his hat on the seat beside him, he leaned forward to rest his elbows on his knees. "Have you met Mr. Anderson?"

"No, I haven't. We married by proxy."

"Is that so? I've never met anyone who married by proxy. Seems sort of risky. Especially for the lady." He wasn't sure why he was questioning her actions. It was none of his business. None at all.

She drew herself up. "I've been swindled before, Mr. Bailey. Cheated by my own flesh and blood, which is precisely why I wished to leave Albany."

A frightened look came over her, tightening her brow. For an instant, she regarded him with widened eyes. The fear vanished as quickly as it had appeared. She pursed her lips and lifted her chin as if reminding herself she was an Astor. Or had once been an Astor. "I'm sorry, Mr. Bailey. I don't know what's come over me. I shouldn't trouble you with silly stories."

He schooled his features into a casual smile. "It's not silly at all. I wish you all the best."

His words weren't exactly heartfelt. Not in the least. He intended to learn more of her circumstances. He told himself it was a work matter. He was a Texas Ranger, after all. A man dedicated to justice and protecting the innocent. The fragile look in her lovely, pale gray eyes had nothing to do with his motives.

Nothing at all.

Chapter Ten

Susanna

The man was imposing, and the scars across his face were like nothing she'd ever seen before, but there was something in his demeanor that hinted at gallant charm. Perhaps a little too much gallant charm. He'd asked to sit in her compartment which seemed a little forward. Not that she could have refused him. It didn't belong to her, unlike her own personal sleeping compartment.

And what had she done to make clear her disapproval? She'd babbled about being swindled. And then she'd proceeded to blather on about a marriage proxy. When she'd finally stopped the words that spilled from her lips, he'd offered his good wishes with a bemused tone.

Which she found a trifle maddening.

After close to a week on the train, she'd concluded that travel brought about a familiarity with other passengers. Strangers offered her sweets, told jokes, or asked about her journey. Children shared their drawings and stories of home.

Close quarters made conversation easy. That didn't mean easy conversation was prudent.

Especially with a tall, imposing lawman. He was handsome enough despite his scars, or perhaps the scars made him more so. She shouldn't think that way about a man's scars. The man must have suffered and that made her heart squeeze with pain. Her preoccupation with this stranger startled her. She tried to deny any sympathetic notions and return to the irritation she'd felt a moment before.

He was arrogant, she decided. He probably made ladies sigh and might be the type to toy with a woman's heart. He had that easy confidence, and his sultry gaze made her uncomfortable. She looked out the window to make clear she wasn't the type who enjoyed flirtatious chit-chat.

There was little to see out the window since they passed through a forested landscape. She resolved to continue her study of the ledger Mr. Anderson had sent, detailing various aspects of the farm. If she could quit stealing glances at him and pay him no mind, he might leave. Keeping her eyes on Mr. Anderson's ledger, she tried her best not to glance his direction. It wasn't easy. She read the same few lines over and over, and try as she might, her gaze drifted toward Mr. Bailey.

She chided herself for giving into her overwhelming curiosity. Why was it suddenly difficult to read her book? Her eyes skimmed the same words over and over. No matter how much she tried to disregard Mr. Bailey, her gaze returned to his masculine form, taking up the opposite corner of the compartment.

To make matters worse, he caught her each time her eyes drifted his way and made it clear he'd caught her with a lifted brow or quirk of his lips.

"Does the gun trouble you?" he asked.

"I'm not troubled. Not by the gun or anything else. Not troubled in the least."

He nodded, his expression solemn. She forced her attention back to her book, managing with extreme difficulty to wade past one line and then one more. With the next sentence, the words blurred.

She gave up on that page and turned to the next in hopes she might find something more interesting. A tapping noise drew her attention. Mr. Bailey drummed his fingers on the armrest. The cad was trying to distract her.

What would Molly do with a man like Mr. Bailey? Probably flirt outrageously. She'd use her feminine wiles, of course. Her aunt spoke glowingly of the charm of Southern men. One of her admirers was from Lafayette, she often recalled wistfully. Pierre proved to be a very gallant gentleman who, at the end of the day, sadly had more manners than money.

Mr. Bailey interrupted her thoughts of Molly. "You probably don't see many guns where you come from."

She noted his Texas drawl, the way he lingered on each vowel as if in no hurry. His voice was a deep baritone. His speech was smooth. She supposed if she could hear his accent, he could hear hers.

"No, not many men walk around Albany with gun belts, Mr. Bailey."

He offered a slow, languid grin. His dark beard contrasted with his white teeth.

"Albany, New York."

"Does that amuse you?" she asked.

"A little."

"Just because a man carries a gun doesn't make him dangerous. Conversely, just because he's unarmed doesn't mean he's not dangerous. Words can be as harmful as weapons."

She congratulated herself on her reply, thinking it summed matters up nicely. With luck, her reply would put an end to the conversation. Mr. Bailey didn't appear to be of the same opinion, however. Instead of politely nodding and letting it be, he grew animated. His brow knit. His lips thinned. He shook his head.

"No, ma'am. I believe you're wrong there."

Ma'am? No one had ever called her that word. *Ma'am...* Was he teasing? He didn't appear to be taunting her. If anything, he appeared quite earnest.

He went on. "I can tell you from experience that words are nowhere near as harmful as bullets."

She set her book aside. "How so? Do you mean to say you've been shot?"

"A few times. The last time was just last month."

She doubted that very much. He seemed to be in robust health.

"Where were you shot?"

"In El Paso."

"I mean where did the bullet hit you?"

He pointed to a spot on his side. "Just below the ribs. It passed right through."

Was he toying with her by recounting such an outlandish tale? She couldn't tell if he was telling the truth. His story of surviving a bullet seemed to give credence to her opinion that words could still be more dangerous than bullets, but it was clear Mr. Bailey wasn't going to concede that point.

"It was just a .22," he said with a shrug.

This was her chance to end the conversation with Mr. Bailey. She should just smile politely and go back to her book. A spark of curiosity burned inside her mind, however.

"A twenty-two?"

"Yes, ma'am."

She wished he'd stop calling her that. In Albany, only elderly ladies were addressed with 'ma'am'. Was she supposed to call him 'sir'? She wouldn't, of course, but wondered if that was how things were done in Texas.

He continued. "That's a pretty small caliber. It can still injure a man. Even kill him. Just the same, there are more dangerous guns."

Her gaze drifted to his gun belt. From the far side of the compartment, she could only see the handle of his gun. The material glinted in the light of the setting sun.

"I always carry a pistol," he offered. "It's part of the job."

She picked up her book. "That's fascinating."

Shifting in her seat, she tilted her book toward the fading sunlight and returned to her reading. Again, she read the same line repeatedly. She kept her gaze fixed on the page, but instead of reading, she rehearsed different ways of asking him to leave her compartment. None seemed quite right. Either they were too forceful or not forceful enough.

A vague disturbance drew her attention. Two men shouted at each other. Angry voices grew louder, drifting down the hallway of the train.

The commotion alarmed her. What worried her even more was the change that came over Mr. Bailey. In an instant, he changed from amiable traveling companion to lethal lawman. He stood and went to the door of the compartment, his movements fluid and stealthy. His transformation startled her, causing her to shrink back in her seat.

He glanced back, his eyes dark as night. "Stay put."

With those words, he was gone.

Stay put? Did Mr. Bailey think he could tell her what to do? Oh, no. She hadn't come all this way to take orders from a man. She'd left that behind in Albany.

And yet, the notion of debating anything with this man made her heart fret.

She tried to avoid arguing with anyone other than Henry. It was safe to argue with him. Their banter always made her smile because Henry was kind and gentle. She never worried he would become angry.

Her father, however, shouted anytime there was a difference of opinion. Which was all the time. When they argued, he grew red-faced and raged at her, making perfectly clear she was not only wrong but also an empty-headed girl. In his opinion, she'd never be anything but a fool.

Susanna felt a jolt of self-pity. Even on a train in Texas, her father's words rang in her mind. She'd left home, but it was as if he'd come with her. It seemed unfair. Would she never escape?

Dear heavens, what if Mr. Bailey shouted like her father? What if he made her trip over her words? The fearful possibilities loomed larger and larger with each passing mile.

Over the next quarter hour, she fidgeted, moved restlessly around the small compartment, and peered out the door a few times. As the train chugged through the woodlands, her mind calmed. Her fears of her father faded. Maybe Mr. Bailey wouldn't come back from his task. That would be ideal. She could return to her books and pretend the entire exchange never happened.

She peeked out the door one last time. At that precise moment, Mr. Bailey strode down the narrow hallway. His broad shoulders practically spanned the width of the hall. She drew a sharp breath. He fixed his gaze on her, clearly displeased that she had not followed his directions to 'stay put'.

He drew closer, stopping a couple of paces from her.

"The sun is setting," he remarked.

"It tends to do that this time of the day." She didn't know where her cheeky response had come from. A few moments ago, she'd imagined her father's enraged screaming and practically collapsed from fear. Her fear had gone, apparently. She could imagine Molly saying something every bit as defiant. She congratulated herself and imagined Molly giving a nod of approval.

"Yes, ma'am."

Infuriating man. She felt a flicker of irritation. At the same time, she noted her confidence notch up a tiny bit. Maybe Mr. Bailey's impossible demeanor could help her overcome her fretfulness.

"Have you had your supper?" he asked.

"I have."

"You'd best head to your cabin. Third class is full of rough types. I just had to stop a few of them from brawling."

She was taken aback. A brawl? But then it dawned on her that the insufferable Mr. Bailey was dismissing her. Sending her to bed as if she were a mere child.

"Mr. Bailey, when I left Albany, it was to escape men who wanted to direct my life. I'll retire when it suits me. Not a moment earlier."

His teeth flashed with a smile. "Fair enough. I'm staying if you are."

"I might read for a good while."

"S'fine."

What did he mean by s'fine? She blinked, trying to piece together what he intended by that curious phrase. Whatever the meaning, it couldn't be good.

Sensing her confusion, he offered an explanation. "You read to your heart's content, and when you're done, I'll see you to your cabin. I'd like to be sure no one troubles you."

His words stunned her. "You intend to escort me to my sleeping compartment?"

"Yes, ma'am."

Ever since she'd boarded the train, the porters and conductors had taken special care of her, especially in the evenings when it was time to turn in. None had offered to go with her to and from her cabin, however.

It seemed scandalous. He was a big, powerful man who intimidated her at first, but now he inspired deep indignation. He was overbearing. Bossy. Impossible. What made it even worse was his dashing, handsome appearance.

"Fine, then. I might as well retire. I don't care to witness any ruffians brawling."

Without waiting for a response, she took her books and made her way down the hall.

With the noise of the train, she wasn't entirely sure he followed. When she glanced back, she found that Mr. Bailey trailed a few paces behind. He continued trailing her down the train. Without a backwards glance, she determined as much from the other passengers. When she passed them, they gave her a cursory glance. Almost at once they directed their attention to a spot behind her, a wary look coming over their features.

Pausing at her cabin, she took her key from her pocketbook. She offered a few polite words of gratitude, intending to send him on his way. Instead of responding, he looked past her, a dark expression in his eyes.

When she followed his gaze to her cabin door, she found it ajar.

"Pardon me, ma'am." Beau nudged her aside and disappeared into her cabin. A commotion ensued. A panicked yelp came from inside her cabin. Beau's deep voice followed.

With the rumble of the train, it was impossible to know what happened within.

What on earth was happening inside her cabin?

Beau appeared a moment later with a sheepish grin. He jabbed his thumb over his shoulder. "The room attendant turned down your bed, Mrs. Anderson."

She nodded. "Y-yes, they do that each night in first class."

"I didn't realize. Rangers don't travel first class."

"My aunt has some connections with the trainline."

The room attendant scurried out of the room, hurrying away without so much as a backwards glance.

"He asked if I'm your husband." Beau chuckled.

Susanna drew a sharp breath. The man must not have the slightest notion of impropriety. He'd just walked into a woman's private cabin without even a second thought. The staff knew she traveled alone.

Molly, with her connections to the train company, had made certain that the staff took care of her every leg of the trip. It was because of Molly that the staff had been especially attentive. What would they think about a stranger prowling her room? A tall, imposing stranger who didn't hesitate to accost the poor room attendant.

The staff probably gossiped about this very kind of thing. They'd imagine her to be a woman with no morals. A woman who freely invited men into her cabin to engage in all manner of dalliances. Dear heavens. She felt lightheaded. Even though she agreed to a marriage of convenience, she still wanted to be thought of as a proper, respectable lady.

Thank goodness she would reach Houston by midday tomorrow. She stared at him with what must be a look of horror.

Beau set his hand on her shoulder and ushered her into her room. "Glad to see you tucked in your room, safe and sound. Close the door now and lock it up."

Slowly, and slightly dazed, she did as she was told. When she slid the bolt across, locking the door, she waited with a foolish sense of expectation. Should she say something? Ignore the man on the other side of the door? What precisely was the etiquette in this sort of situation? Fervently, she hoped the staff noted Mr. Bailey had left her cabin.

She leaned towards the door, pressing her ear to the wood panel. When his voice sounded, not more than an inch or two away, she jumped.

"You have a good evening, Mrs. Anderson," he said.

She set her palm on the door, imagining him just on the other side. His tone was partway between bemused and domineering. There was something else there too, a note of concern.

Earlier, while talking with him in the compartment, his demeanor had galled her. Now she tried to ignore his bossy ways. What was the use objecting to his manners? Mr. Bailey was a man who did as he pleased. He had a distinct air of quiet authority and she didn't want to challenge him again, not even from behind a bolted door.

"Yes, well, good night," she replied.

His chuckle, so close to her ear, sent a jolt of awareness across her senses. She rested her forehead on the door and thought about the man on the other side. He was a gruff lawman unlike any she'd ever known. One she'd likely never see again. Had he already left? She waited, her breath stilled in her throat.

"I hope you rest well." She cringed at her words, half-hoping he hadn't heard. She was never so familiar with a stranger. What on earth had come over her?

"Thank you," he said.

She thought she heard a smile in his voice when he added, "I hope you rest well too, ma'am."

Chapter Eleven

Beau

There was a reason the best Rangers in Texas were unmarried. Women were a distraction. This was a fact that was made clear around midnight.

Beau had found a spot a few paces from Susanna Anderson's sleeping compartment. It was a small alcove, out of the way of passengers. From there he could watch her door without drawing attention to himself.

Ever since he bid her good night, he'd wrestled with thoughts of the copper-haired girl.

She was refined. Far too fancy to live on a ranch in Sweet Willow. The notion was almost as outrageous as her marrying one of the Anderson men. His thoughts drifted from disbelief to concern. What if her husband had passed? What if both Anderson men had passed?

And this was when the trouble began. With his mind preoccupied by the Anderson woman, he didn't notice the shadows in the hallway, or not right off. Two men stopped at her door. They crouched, leaned together and spoke. Beau couldn't hear the words over the din of the train. The glint of a knife flashed as one of them tried to pry open the lock of her door.

Beau hardly cared who they were. He was no longer even thinking of the Craddicks. Without conscious thought, he moved stealthily, closing the distance between him and the men in a few quick strides.

After that, his years of Ranger work took over. Without a word of questioning, he presumed guilt of the men. It was an easy decision. They were trying to gain entry to the compartment of an unaccompanied female.

Beau gripped the head of the nearest man, using it to strike the head of the other. In an instant, both men fell. They lay unmoving in the narrow aisle. He lit a match and confirmed their identity.

The train wouldn't arrive in Houston till morning which left Beau with a small dilemma. What to do with the men for the rest of the night. He solved the problem by dragging them to the alcove.

The Craddick brothers had grown stout since taking up robbing train passengers. It wasn't an easy task to move them into the small space. Fortunately, they were out cold. Using their belts, he restrained the men, tying their hands behind their backs. He propped them against the back of the alcove and waited for morning.

The rest of the night passed without incident. The men didn't stir until past daybreak. They groaned and shifted and promptly passed out again. Usually, Beau enjoyed a small sense of accomplishment when he collared a criminal. He'd just captured two outlaws, but he hardly noted even a glimmer of satisfaction. Instead, he mulled over what would happen to Susanna Anderson if her husband had passed.

The train slowed as it approached the Houston depot. Beau gave orders that no passengers were to disembark until he'd given the all-clear. The train screeched to a halt, steam hissing from the wheels. From a nearby door, Beau signaled to a group of waiting Rangers who dragged the outlaws from the train.

Captain Maddox, who was there each time Beau returned to Houston, nodded. Unsmiling as always. "Finally."

"Yes, sir. Finally."

"What now?" Captain Maddox asked. "I don't need an extra man, even if he is the notorious Beau Bailey."

Under other circumstances, Beau might have sparred with the man. Not that morning, however. He had other things on his mind.

"I'm requesting time to take care of a personal matter, sir."

The captain nodded. Beau wasn't sure if the man was relieved to be rid of him, or merely surprised by the request.

"Granted. I'll send word to Austin that I've allowed you to take two weeks of leave."

Beau thanked him and bid him goodbye. Returning to the train, he considered the turn of events. A couple of weeks! He hadn't had that kind of leave since joining the Rangers. He'd spend it in Sweet Willow, with one of his cousins. It would allow him to learn more about Mrs. Anderson's situation.

He spoke to the train engineer, giving the go-ahead for passengers to disembark.

People began unloading. Beau found Mrs. Anderson in her cabin. The porter had stacked and readied her belongings by the door. She stood nearby, dressed in a blue dress, hat, and shawl. He couldn't help an admiring glance but quickly assumed an all-business demeanor, removing his hat as he greeted her.

"Good morning, Mr. Bailey. The porter has told me there's no one waiting in the first-class arrivals."

Her face was pale, her features taut. Standing beside her trunks, she looked delicate, even fragile, not like yesterday when she'd bristled at most everything he said. He felt a pang of sympathy. How difficult and frightening it must be for a woman traveling alone. She'd probably fretted all the way to Texas. And now she was finally here but there was no one to meet her, to welcome her and offer a kind word after a long journey. It seemed cruel.

She went on. "He also told me two men were arrested, right here on the train."

"Yes, ma'am. I made the arrest." He didn't explain that he'd apprehended the men just a few paces away.

"I'll find some way to Sweet Willow. Surely there's a coach I can hire. The porter promised to ask."

"I'll take you, Mrs. Anderson."

Her lips parted with surprise.

He didn't blame her. Heck, he felt a tad surprised at his own words.

While he felt strongly about making sure that Mrs. Anderson was safely settled in Sweet Willow, he hadn't imagined *taking* her. There were several reasons why that was a poor idea. She'd likely object to traveling with a stranger. Any sensible woman *ought* to object to such a thing.

Beau gritted his teeth. The Anderson fella didn't deserve Susanna. Unless he was deceased, of course. In that case he had an excuse for not coming. Beau decided against suggesting that particular possibility. Mrs. Anderson looked to be very close to tears and he didn't want to add to her misery.

"You would take me to Sweet Willow?" she asked softly.

"That's what I said, isn't it?"

He regretted his gruff tone, but either she did not notice or did not mind his brusque response. Instead, she seemed to consider his offer, eyeing him warily. Her gaze drifted to the luggage, a considerable pile of trunks and bags.

"I'd be happy to take you," he added in what he hoped was a more conciliatory voice. "It seems poor manners that Mr.

Anderson didn't meet you at the end of such a long journey. A husband ought not to treat his wife with such disregard."

Her eyes lit with a spark of interest as if she'd never considered such a notion. "I'm sure many husbands treat their wives with some disregard at times."

"Not husbands who cherish their wives."

To his surprise, her lips tilted with the hint of a smile. Surprising. She was making a small recovery from her distress. Many women would be crying by this point. Susanna Anderson was no fragile female, he noted with approval. This attribute would serve in her favor if she had traveled all the way to Sweet Willow only to discover she was a widow.

"I would very much like to take your offer, Mr. Bailey." Her cheeks colored a lovely pink. "Although I hate to impose."

"No imposition."

"I could pay you for your time."

He frowned. "As a Ranger, it's my duty to serve and protect."

"Your duty?"

"That's right."

"So you'd do this for anyone?"

He arched a brow. "Yes. Although some duties are more pleasant than others."

She blushed. A shy smile tugged at her lips as she put on her hat and gloves. He ushered her out of the train, instructed the porter to tote her things to the platform and got a buckboard from the livery.

Mrs. Anderson watched quietly, taking in the men loading her things on the back of the wagon as well as the sights of the train station.

He helped her to the wagon seat and drove the buckboard out of the bustle of the station and the Houston streets.

"I hope nothing has happened to Mr. Anderson," she said as they turned on the road to Sweet Willow. "I confess that I've worried all the way to Texas."

Beau considered her words, trying not to imagine the moment when he'd deliver Mrs. Anderson to her elderly husband.

"I suppose you could return to New York."

"Certainly not."

He suppressed a smile. The haughty tone from yesterday had returned. "If something happened to Mr. Anderson, you couldn't manage a ranch on your own."

She didn't even flinch at his words.

"And why not, Mr. Bailey? If an elderly man can manage, I assume I would find a way. I have to go to the ranch to make sure his nephew doesn't take the land and more importantly to take care of the donkeys."

He turned to look at her. What on earth was she talking about? Donkeys? "Ma'am?"

She knit her brow but said nothing.

"Did you just say you needed to take care of donkeys?"

A sheepish look came over her. "Mr. Anderson has a few donkeys he cares for. I have the impression they're very dear to him. They'd been mistreated before he took them in. He wants to be certain the animals are cared for. I sent a note, promising to take care of them."

She lifted her gaze to meet his before looking away shyly. "I have to believe that was one of the reasons he sent off for a bride. He wrote that he didn't seek romance."

"You mean a marriage in name only?"

Her color deepened. She gave him a prim look without answering.

"You've come to Texas to care for a bunch of donkeys?"

"Caring for a bunch of donkeys appeals to me. Especially when I consider the alternative."

"Which is?"

"Being forced to wed the man my father wanted me to marry."

"Are you saying..." Beau's words trailed off. He frowned. "That your father doesn't know you're here?"

"No, but he won't care. If I'm not around to cause trouble about my inheritance, I could have run away with a traveling circus."

Beau grumbled and shook his head. With each passing mile, his discontent grew. What had he gotten himself into? Even worse, what had she gotten herself into? He glanced at her gloved hands, trying to imagine how a girl who wore kid gloves could possibly take on ranch work.

Mr. Anderson had sent for a bride out of pure spite. He didn't care who came, so long as his property stayed out of the hands of his kinfolk. To top things off, the man might have passed on or might very soon. Susanna would be on her own. Beau couldn't decide which possibility he disliked more – Susanna marrying that ornery old codger, or Susanna living alone on a desolate ranch.

"They're named after the angels," she said, a smile tugging at the corners of her mouth.

"Beg your pardon?"

"The three donkeys." Her eyes sparkled. "I admit, when he told me about them, I felt a sense of possibility, a sense of very real excitement. I've never been allowed to have a pet. I can hardly wait to meet Gabriel, Michael and Rafael."

Beau gathered the reins in one hand and rubbed the back of his neck with the other. His shoulders felt tight with tension he hadn't noticed earlier. He groaned with a sudden desire to turn the buckboard around and take her far away from the ordeal that awaited her. Anywhere but Sweet Willow.

He disliked the idea of her marrying anyone, much less an old surly man. The more she spoke of her situation, the more he disliked everything about it. She'd left her family without their knowing. She'd agreed to marry a man three times her age. And to top it off, if her husband had passed away, she planned on taking care of everything, including a bunch of cantankerous critters.

He scowled at her. "Mrs. Anderson, have you ever *met* a donkey?"

"Never."

"This should be very, very interesting."

She gave a breathless laugh. "It most assuredly will. I don't see it as a hardship, Mr. Bailey."

"How do you see it?"

Her smile faded, she lifted her gray eyes to look into his, a solemn gaze that made him catch his breath.

She spoke softly. "A blessing."

The girl was so innocent, so wide-eyed, he felt a pang deep in his chest. He hoped he wasn't delivering her to a terrible situation. The possibilities were numerous, but the worst would be the prospect of being a widow.

"I know what you're thinking," she said, her tone bright.

His brows shot up. That her intended had passed? Now, that would be the biggest surprise yet.

She continued. "You think this is a risk. That I'm desperate. And I'll admit I felt some degree of desperation, but I could have gone other places to avoid the marriage my father planned. I wanted to come here because I saw how I could not only help myself but also another person."

94

"I understand." Not really, but he was trying to be agreeable.

"So often we can only get something if we deprive another person. I feel it's a blessing to be able to both give and receive."

Her response was a tad different than what he'd expected.

She smiled gently. "It might sound silly, but I felt called to come to Texas."

He didn't think that was silly. Not at all. They rode in silence until he found the words to reply. "I'm sure things will work out the way they were meant to, Mrs. Anderson. I reckon it's just a matter of having faith in God's plan."

Her smile broadened. "He does work in mysterious ways."

Chapter Twelve

Susanna

The wagon creaked as they crested the last hill. Mr. Bailey stopped the team and pointed out the Anderson ranch in the green valley below. Susanna's breath caught as she set her hand on her heart and took in the astonishing sight. The assortment of buildings meant little to her. Instead, she admired the land. It stretched from a distant ridge, narrowed to a verdant dale, bordered by a stream. A broad, shimmering river ran along the other side of the ranch.

"I've never seen such a beautiful sky. Or such a horizon. Oh, my, but it's beautiful."

Mr. Bailey snapped the reins and the horses proceeded down the hill.

As they drew closer, she noted the clusters of trees here and there. Mr. Anderson had spoken with pride of the immense oak trees on his land, and how his nephew conspired to cut them down and sell the lumber. He told of the peach orchard he and his brother planted, and of the fruit they bore each summer.

A small cabin sat a short distance from the other structures, a thin spiral of smoke swirling from the chimney. Her heart quickened when she considered the smoke came from a fire in a hearth. Had Mr. Anderson set the fire in that fireplace? Did the poor lonesome fellow wait for a companion? A helpmeet?

She'd never known meaningful work. While she had always kept busy, she'd simply done as she pleased and had little to show for her life. Here, on this land, she might actually do something useful. God-willing.

Praying yet again for a new beginning, she squared her shoulders and summoned her courage. She wouldn't dwell on questions or fears. Instead, she took in the details of the majestic beauty of the land. It was lovely, vast and so unlike any she'd known. A pang of loneliness struck her heart. She would have dearly loved to share this sight with Molly and, of course, Henry.

"Are you ready for this?" Mr. Bailey asked quietly.

"I am." She'd tried to sound lighthearted, but her voice wavered.

He drove to the cabin with smoke coming from the chimney. The house was tidy with yellow curtains in the windows. Colorful flowers grew in the beds surrounding the home and an immense garden filled the plot nearby. Two women appeared, followed closely by a young man, his expression solemn. He looked to be about fourteen or so, tall, gangly, earnest but awkward too.

"Afternoon," Mr. Bailey called.

The boy stepped to the forefront. "Good morning, sir."

The boy addressed Mr. Bailey, but his gaze was fixed firmly on Susanna. "Mrs. Anderson?"

"That's right. I am Susanna Anderson."

He gave her a polite nod. "My name is Oscar Novak." He gestured to the ladies. "My mother, Elsa, and grandmother, Victoria."

Mr. Bailey helped her down from the buckboard and introduced himself. "Where's Mr. Anderson?"

The boy swallowed hard, his throat constricting with the effort. His wide eyes flashed with apprehension as his gaze shifted from Susanna to Mr. Bailey and back again.

The older of the two women murmured a few words. It was a language Susanna didn't recognize. Both women were fair, with light eyes, and Susanna might have guessed German but she knew that wasn't right. If they'd spoken in German, she might have known a word or two.

"My family works for Mr. Anderson," Oscar said. "I'm sorry to tell you that he passed away."

Susanna's heart dropped. She swayed on unsteady legs. Mr. Bailey came to her side, clasped her arm in his.

"Steady, there."

Robert was gone...

A breeze blew softly. Distantly, she heard the mew of a cat. Mr. Bailey tightened his hold as he coaxed her to the cabin. Susanna was unaware of what happened next, but soon found herself inside the cabin, sitting before the fireplace.

She stared into the fire that burned in the grate. The younger woman set a cup of tea on the table beside her. The older woman took a nearby chair and sat silently while the other added wood to the fire.

Mr. Bailey and Oscar remained outside, tending to the horse and wagon. The jangle of the harnesses faded.

Susanna's tumultuous thoughts slowed. Molly had guessed such a thing might happen. Susanna had to admit the possibility, of course. Mr. Anderson was elderly. But in her mind, she'd pictured arriving to his home, spending time with him and perhaps getting at least somewhat acquainted.

At the least, she hoped to learn more about the homestead. More than the instructions in the ledger. The land. The animals. Robert Anderson had left behind enough property and livestock to fill the pages of a ledger. The task before her seemed to loom ominously. He was gone. She was alone. Where should she begin? She had no idea.

Over the next hour, the Novak ladies showed her Robert's home, which was now hers, she realized with disbelief. The little house had been built in stages. First, the parlor, kitchen and a small, narrow bedroom. After that it seemed that Robert, or someone, had added a room here, and a room there as the notion struck them.

The result was a warren of rooms and narrow halls. Robert's room lay at the end of one of the halls. Old ledgers and newspapers lay scattered across every surface. The ladies apologized for the untidiness.

Robert didn't mind disorder in his home. Despite that, he'd clearly put some thought into a place for Susanna. He'd picked a sunny, cheerful room on the east side of the cabin. It had a spacious wardrobe and a large, four-poster bed.

Beau and Oscar unloaded the trunks that held her clothing. There was no room in the house for her books. Robert Anderson didn't have any books or shelves. Susanna could hardly imagine a house without books, but it couldn't be helped. Not yet. For now, she needed to store her precious books in the barn.

The women helped her unpack her clothes. Susanna wanted to see the property, especially the three donkeys, but the Novak ladies were determined to see her settled in the house.

Once Victoria Novak got something in her mind, she wasn't easy to refuse. Susanna went along with their plan. She resolved to ask Oscar to show her the animals when they were done unpacking her trunks.

The ladies had given her a quilt as a wedding gift, something that was a tradition in the Novak family.

"We made it for you when we found the letters from the agency in New York," Elsa said, shyly. "There was no time to make something fancy."

Susanna stood at the foot of the bed and admired the handiwork. "It's lovely. I hardly know what to say to such a generous gesture."

The older woman, Victoria, waved a dismissive hand. "Robert's blankets were no good. He kept everything, no matter how old or broken."

Susanna had to agree with her. She opened a few of the drawers and found odd assortments of pencil nubs, candle remnants, corks and a jar of spent matches. He kept buttons even if they were broken. Nails, both bent and straight.

"Robert was a little mixed up," Elsa said as she tucked a few of Susanna's shawls into a drawer. "It was maybe a little worse after his brother died."

"Tell me about Robert," Susanna said softly. "Was he a nice man?"

Elsa replied. "He was good to us. Very kind to Oscar. My son has a broken heart now."

"He misses Mr. Anderson?" Susanna murmured. "Of course. A boy needs a father."

"I think so too," Elsa replied.

"His nephew wants this ranch. He come to the ranch, saying it belong to him," Victoria said with contempt. "We tell him about you. We try to send him away. Oscar lock the barn and tell the sheriff in Sweet Willow."

Susanna stopped her task of folding a muslin frock. "Jack was here?"

Victoria didn't immediately answer. She took the last of Susanna's shoes from a trunk and set them in the wardrobe. Elsa nodded in reply to the question.

Susanna's blood chilled in her veins. She'd known all along that Jack Anderson would be a threat but assumed Robert would help her confront him. She realized that now that she'd pictured working together with Robert on everything, not just the trouble of a greedy nephew. Not once had she imagined being widowed before she even met her husband.

A fresh wave of overwhelming exhaustion came over her. She'd come all this way only to find men like her father and Edgar Wiggins were everywhere. Even worse, she didn't have Henry or Aunt Molly to rely on.

"You need husband," Victoria said.

Elsa made a scoffing sound. "Another husband? Mrs. Anderson is a widow. How can she marry again?"

The two women began an animated conversation in Czech. Susanna wondered if the argument pertained to her but couldn't imagine how. There seemed to be some long-standing contention between the women. The squabble grew in volume, but when Elsa gestured toward Susanna, the women abruptly stopped their quarrel. They looked remorseful and continued working quietly and diligently.

A few minutes later, Elsa spoke. "You can marry Mr. Bailey."

"I beg your pardon?" Susanna recoiled.

Victoria nodded. "Bailey family are good people."

Susanna unpacked her brushes and hair combs, setting them on a table under the window. "A moment ago, Elsa said widows shouldn't marry. Now you have me wedding a lawman I barely know."

Elsa smiled. Victoria waved a dismissive hand, but Susanna was certain the older woman's mouth hinted at a smile.

"You didn't know Mr. Anderson," Elsa pointed out.

"That's true," Susanna admitted.

"Mr. Bailey is a man of..." Victoria gestured in the air as if trying to grasp the word she needed. She spoke a few words to Elsa.

Elsa nodded. "A man of honor."

"True," Susanna said. "He's impossible and arrogant and overbearing but he is honorable."

Susanna considered the Novak's good opinion of Beau and the Bailey family. It came as no surprise that Beau came from a good family. He'd been very gallant and kind to her. She was sure the rest of the Baileys were every bit as fine as Beau, but that hardly mattered. Even if she wanted a husband, Beau wasn't the marrying type.

Elsa and Victoria moved to the window. Susanna went to their side. Beau worked with Oscar, splitting wood. Beau had taken on the task, probably because it needed doing. He swung the ax, bringing it down on a piece of wood, chopping it neatly into two. The pieces tumbled to the ground.

Beau set another log in place and handed the ax to Oscar who took it without a word. Susanna marveled at the ease between the two. The man and the boy had only met. And yet there was an easy familiarity between them clear in the way they worked.

She drew away from the window. "I'm not marrying anyone, certainly not Mr. Bailey. He's leaving. Soon. Maybe today."

The women turned, uttering words of dismay. "But the nephew. He will return. And he'll take the rest of Mr. Anderson's animals."

"The *rest* of the animals?" Susanna asked with dismay.

The women nodded.

Victoria frowned. "He knows Mr. Anderson love his animals. He take the donkeys first."

"The donkeys are gone?" Susanna said the shocking words, sinking to the bed.

Victoria paled. "He came in the night. We didn't know. We didn't hear him. He left a note to say the property belongs to him. He take the donkeys to the auction. He would come back with other men and take the rest."

Elsa spoke. "He took the donkeys to the Bailey Auction. It's owned by Mr. Bailey's cousin, Noah."

Susanna hardly knew what to say to all this. All she could think about was the donkeys. The three little creatures that had been so dear to Robert Anderson.

"You must be careful," Elsa said, coming to her side.

The news shocked Susanna. It seemed that everything she'd planned had been turned on its head. She shook her head with despair. "I've just arrived and already I've failed the single thing Robert Anderson asked of me."

Chapter Thirteen

Beau

Oscar took Beau around the Anderson farmyard, showing him the barn, a couple of open-facing sheds, the orchards down the lane and the various pastures. Mr. Anderson leased the pastures to neighbors for grazing, but only in the winter. Robert Anderson didn't approve of overgrazing.

The boy had admired the man. That much was clear. A few times his eyes welled with tears when he spoke of spending time with Mr. Anderson. Beau got the feeling the boy wasn't telling him the whole story, however. He seemed agitated and tight-lipped about some details of the ranch.

They walked the path back to the house.

"I'd always heard he was disagreeable," Beau said.

Oscar nodded. "Sometimes."

"Well, he left behind a nice place here."

The boy grew quiet.

As they approached Mr. Anderson's cabin, they passed an identical one with blue curtains and flowerpots on the porch. Oscar gestured to the building. "My grandmother said you will stay here."

"Did she?" Beau suppressed a grin.

"You will stay?" Oscar asked.

"I was thinking about it. I need to convince Susanna."

"Mr. Anderson left a note about signing something called a proxy."

"That's right. A marriage proxy."

"This means she owns the ranch. No one can take it from her?"

"That's right."

This seemed to appease the boy. The worry in his eyes faded.

Beau eyed the other home, the one that had belonged to Mr. Anderson. The three women worked inside, getting Susanna settled. He tried to imagine Susanna unpacking her fancy clothes and fine things in Robert Anderson's home. Did the house seem rustic and rough to her?

Part of him wanted to stop her from unpacking. She couldn't possibly stay on. How would she manage? And how would he be able to leave a young, untested city girl to fend for herself with a ranch to run? The Novaks were kind and dedicated, but they were only two women and a youth. They needed a man to take care of things.

A wagon came up the road, a buckboard pulled by a sturdy pair of matched bays. Beau thought he recognized the man driving. Oscar gave a sigh, as if he too recognized the man and wasn't terribly pleased to see him.

"Is that Fritz Weber? The fella who owns the mercantile?"

"Yes, sir," Oscar said with a note of scorn.

"Beau!" Fritz called, pulling the horses to a halt. "What a surprise."

He climbed down from the wagon and the men shook hands. Fritz greeted Oscar with a friendly pat on the shoulder before returning his attention to Beau.

"I read about you in the newspaper. Very glad you were able to arrest those three men. What a story! Three at once."

The darned Fort Worth newspaper story. He had no idea if it was a reprint of the same story or a new rendition. Either way, it wasn't a good thing. Rangers needed to have stealth on their side. Notoriety and recognition were bad for business.

Beau could feel Oscar's surprised gaze on him.

"Just part of the job," Beau said.

"And you're staying here to keep Mr. Anderson's nephew away?"

Beau shook his head. "I met Susanna Anderson on the train. I brought her to Sweet Willow since I had the time, but I'll have to report back to work in two weeks."

Fritz nodded, confusion clouding his eyes. "Ach, I thought this was part of your work. Maybe since Jack Anderson has been causing problems. Selling the old man's donkeys. Saying he won't let a woman take his uncle's land."

Beau frowned. Oscar hadn't told him any of that. One glance at the boy's wide eyes told him all he needed to know. Jack must have come to the farm and frightened the boy. Maybe the women too.

Oscar looked guilt-ridden and distraught.

"We didn't know about Susanna at first," said the boy. "When Jack Anderson came to the ranch, he said the place belonged to him." Oscar blinked back the tears. "When my grandmother told him about Mr. Anderson's mail-order bride, he got very mad. He came in the night and took the donkeys to the auction yard."

Fritz looked taken aback. "Ja, I'm sorry Oscar. I know you're a good boy. I think what you need here is a good dog, heh? A hound that will let you know a stranger has arrived."

Oscar looked like he wanted to kick someone, probably Fritz. Beau took his hat off, raked his fingers through his hair and set it back on, trying to piece together the new

107

information. He wasn't sure what the problem was between Oscar and Fritz, but a more important problem was the Anderson nephew, and that wasn't even the worst of it. The nephew had sold off the donkeys. He knew Susanna would take the news hard.

The women came out of Mr. Anderson's cabin. One look at Susanna told Beau she knew about the donkeys. She looked pale and stricken. The Novak ladies looked displeased as well. But the frown on Elsa Novak's face, Oscar's mother, quickly changed when she saw Mr. Weber. She stole furtive looks at Mr. Weber who smiled back.

Beau frowned at the scene before him.

Fritz gazed at Elsa. Victoria Novak glared at Fritz. Susanna looked ill and Oscar looked even angrier than his grandmother.

Beau let out a heavy sigh, unsure what to make of any of it.

Fritz turned to Oscar. "Tell your mother and grandmother I've come to pay my respects."

Beau frowned. Why was Fritz Weber asking Oscar to speak on his behalf? To his surprise, Oscar started jabbering in Czech. The Novak ladies listened, the elder with a severe expression, the younger with a smile playing upon her lips. Fritz took a basket from the back of the buckboard and gave it to Oscar.

Grandma Novak said a few words in Czech.

Oscar turned to Fritz. "My grandmother says it was a lot of trouble for you."

Fritz shrugged and tousled the boy's hair. Oscar ducked his head and retreated a few steps. Fritz didn't seem to notice and went on in a cheerful tone. "It was nothing. I always liked

Robert Anderson. And I know how much he meant to the Novak family."

Grandma Novak took the basket from Oscar with a brittle nod of thanks. Oscar introduced Susanna to Fritz. Susanna managed to regain her composure well enough to give a gracious greeting.

Beau turned to the shopkeeper and spoke in a low tone. "Would you mind telling folks in town that I'm staying here? I'd like word to get out just in case Jack Anderson has any plans of causing any more trouble."

"I will make sure to say this to people. He won't come back if she has a lawman out here."

"Thank you."

"Especially a man who can arrest three outlaws, by himself." Fritz chuckled.

Beau winced. "Well, I try not to draw attention to myself, but in this case, it might help matters."

Fritz said goodbye and was on his way.

The Novak ladies squabbled over the basket as they returned to Mr. Anderson's cabin. Oscar trudged after them, kicking rocks and clumps of dirt along the way.

Susanna crossed the farmyard as she gazed at Beau with dismay.

"I know. I heard about the donkeys."

"Do you think I can get them back?"

"I can ask around."

She let out a murmur of relief. "I don't know how to thank you."

"If I find them, you can thank me by hiring a foreman. Or maybe selling this place to... oh, I don't know, maybe a rancher."

She shook her head. "Never mind then. I don't think I want your help."

She lifted her chin a notch, quickly recovering from the news of the pilfered donkeys. He noted the determined set of her jaw. She was having no part of his suggestion. The stubborn girl intended to remain and become a rancher, thank you very much.

How would a young woman, accustomed to wealth and privilege, manage a ranch? Clad in a fancy dress trimmed with lace, she looked like she was on her way to lunch with the ladies.

Even her boots were fussy, delicate finely made things, probably kid leather or whatever rich girls from Albany wore.

"Susanna, you need to find a hired man to help you with the ranch. Maybe I can ask my cousins if they know of a decent fellow."

"I don't need a man's help."

He gritted his teeth. Susanna was the most obstinate woman he'd ever met. The realization didn't make the situation any better.

In a few days' time, he'd ride away, leaving her to her own devices. There was nothing about Susanna that was suited to running a ranch. The thought troubled him deeply.

He couldn't imagine Susanna negotiating matters with tradesmen, workers or other ranchers. Another thought disturbed him even more. Even if Jack didn't give her any trouble, other men would see a pretty, single woman and make plans. They'd court her, not just because she was attractive, but because she owned a valuable ranch.

And Beau had to admit the Anderson place was a fine ranch. He wandered past the cabin, intending to ignore

Susanna and her stubborn ways. Instead of going after her and arguing with her, he admired the land a little more.

The Anderson brothers might have been eccentric and set in their ways, but they knew about caring for the land. The lush pastures had clearly been tended. The men had planted grass for cattle, removed scrub brush and cactus, maintained the fences and most important of all, let the fields rest.

Beau admired the sight. The grass swayed in the early evening breezes. The late afternoon sun gave the green grass a golden hue. Wind moved over the pasture, rippling the grass like an expanse of ocean. It left a soft rustle in its wake.

Susanna came to his side. "Did Oscar mention where Robert is buried?" she asked quietly.

Her question drew him from his thoughts. "He said there's a family plot near the stream."

"Would you take me?"

He sighed. "All right."

He led her down the path. The Anderson family plot lay amidst a grove of majestic oaks. The stream flowed a few paces beyond the trees, the fading sun casting a bright glitter across the surface.

A dozen or so gravestones marked the final resting spots of the Anderson clan.

"Oscar told me they had a pastor out to conduct services," Beau said.

"It's so pretty here. I'm glad he has a peaceful spot."

Beau had to agree. Long ago, one of the Anderson men must have noticed the natural beauty here on the riverbank. Beau's gaze drifted to the attention given to the enclosure. It was no ordinary picket fence. Instead, an ornate, wrought-iron fence marked the perimeter.

Susanna's eyes misted as she drew near. She pressed her lips together. Resting her hands on the wrought-iron railing, she gazed at the various headstones. After a moment of silence, she bowed her head in prayer.

Beau chided himself for his poor manners, snatched his hat and closed his eyes to offer prayers for Robert Anderson, for while he didn't know the man, he wanted to pray the man was at peace.

After he finished, he waited respectfully for Susanna to finish with her prayers. He took in a little more of the serene spot beside the stream. Without a word, he wandered around the family plot to the water's edge. The late afternoon sun shone across the shallows, glittering across the surface. The brook flowed over the rocks. A breeze rustled through the oak limbs.

"Robert, I want to say that I'm very sorry," Susanna spoke the words in a clear voice.

Beau parted his lips with surprise. Who could she be talking to? He glanced around, searching for another person he might not have noticed. They were, of course, utterly alone.

He returned his attention to Susanna. Waiting, wondering, he blinked as he watched the young woman struggle with a storm of emotion.

She hadn't moved from the wrought-iron fence. She gazed at the graves with a heartfelt expression, her hands clasped before her. "I promise to do as you ask. To care for the property and the animals. I shall not rest until the donkeys have returned."

The wind stirred the oak branches again. Susanna drew a sharp breath, then gave him a sheepish look.

Susanna wanted to come to the grave so she could apologize to Robert Anderson...

Beau had expected tears, or despair or anything other than an apology and a proclamation to do better. Susanna might be every bit as eccentric as the Anderson men. Despite that, he couldn't help admiring her.

The wind blew a strand of hair across her neck.

That morning, she'd arranged her hair in an elegant fashion, but over the course of the day it had tumbled from the pins and lay across her narrow shoulders. He couldn't help admiring the color and the texture of the lovely disarray. The auburn tendril contrasted with her pale skin.

A smile tugged at his lips as his thoughts drifted. An urge to brush the delicate tress from her neck came over him. He wondered if Susanna's hair felt as soft as it looked.

She gave him a prim look and began her way back to the house, or so he supposed. Who could know what Susanna Anderson intended to do next?

"We all done here?" he called, following a few paces behind.

"Done with what?" she asked, speaking over her shoulder.

"Done chatting with Robert?"

She continued walking. He noted the way her shoulders stiffened. Her pace quickened.

He caught up to her easily enough. She kept her gaze fixed ahead, refusing so much as to even glance his direction.

"You and Robert finished catching up?"

Her cheeks became tinged with pink.

"I hope he didn't give a few dozen more things for your to-do list. That would be pretty thoughtless. If you ask me."

"I didn't ask you."

"Did he say anything at all? Oh, I don't know. Happy to see you. Sorry I didn't get to the station. Also sorry about cutting out on you like I did. Turning up dead and whatnot."

She kept her stormy silence.

When they reached the big house, she stopped abruptly, whirling to face him. He strode past a step or two before he realized she was no longer beside him. He slowed and circled back, coming to a halt a couple of paces from her.

She folded her arms. "It is hardly a mystery you've never married."

She gave him what looked like an attempt to be snooty. Or maybe it was her trying to look sociable. Hard to tell. She schooled her features to offer a cool smile, a smile that didn't quite make it up to her eyes. Her eyes hadn't gotten the message about looking friendly, judging by the way they flashed with anger.

"You think everything about me is humorous, don't you?"

"Well..." His attention drifted to her lips. "Not everything."

"I have been blessed with a chance to make a new life here in Texas. Mr. Anderson asked for very little in return and I have *already* failed him. I feel a strong sense of duty." She set a delicate, gloved hand over her heart. "As a woman who has been disappointed by people I trusted, I feel my responsibility deeply."

A note of pain in her voice made him grimace. He wondered if she mistrusted him along with the other people she alluded to. The notion galled him. He wasn't accustomed to folks doubting him. Even more aggravating was the fact that with each passing moment, she seemed to view Robert Anderson with more respect.

He wanted to point out that he'd helped out a *little* more than her late husband.

"I will help you. I'm sure we can find three donkeys around here somewhere."

A flicker of doubt drifted behind her eyes. "I don't want three donkeys, Beau. I want *those* three donkeys, the three animals that belonged to Robert."

"Of course. I should have known. I will find Robert's donkeys. And I will bring them home for you."

Figuring that was more than enough to make her happy, he waited for a word of thanks. None came. Instead, she still wanted to negotiate the agreement.

She softened her tone. "Can I come with you?"

Take Susanna? He stared in disbelief, hoping she'd give some sign she was joshing.

He didn't know where to begin his search. He could imagine combing the countryside, searching for the critters, stopping at various homes in Sweet Willow, knocking on doors.

Wouldn't he be a sight? A respected Texas Ranger searching not for outlaws. Oh, no. That would be what folks might expect. Instead, he'd be searching for three ornery donkeys named after the angels.

He closed his eyes and sighed deeply, trying to suppress a groan. He opened them to find her gazing up at him, her pretty gray eyes filled with sweet yearning. Her gaze unraveled his rule about working alone. The last thing he wanted to do was carry out this ridiculous errand with a woman tagging along. Try as he might, he couldn't deny her.

"All right, Susanna." He nodded. "I'll take you with me."

"When will we go?"

"How about tomorrow, Mrs. Anderson?" He spoke in an overly polite tone.

"That would be lovely."

Her lips tilted with a grateful smile. He shouldn't be so affected by her smile. He'd never cared about pleasing a young lady. It was unfortunate. Uncanny and regrettable that the first young lady he wanted to make smile happened to be the most uppity, impossible female he'd ever met.

Chapter Fourteen

Oscar

That night, Oscar lay in his bed, listening to his mother and grandmother. From the loft of the cabin he could always hear their evening conversations perfectly. Usually, he was too tired to listen to the women's talk, but not tonight.

He was happy that Susanna had come. And Beau. But he wasn't happy about other things. Nothing was as bad as the missing donkeys, of course, but Mr. Weber's visit that afternoon troubled him. Now that the man had come to visit, he might see fit to do so again. And then again.

Not only had he visited, but he'd left a basket. It contained some sweets, a cake from the German bakery and apples. He'd also left something for Oscar's mother. More ribbon for her hair.

Babka fussed about the ribbon. She insisted that Mama should not accept such a personal gift. It wasn't right. The German man would think she liked him. Oscar found himself nodding in agreement with Babka, a rare occurrence.

Mama said it was just ribbon. Nothing more.

Oscar heard the way his mother said the words and knew perfectly well the gift was more than just ribbon. He could tell from the soft tone she used. Babka must not have noticed the way she spoke. Oscar knew though. His mother liked Mr. Weber.

He yanked the blanket over his shoulder. Babka also didn't know that Mr. Weber had given ribbon to Mama before. Or that he thought her hair looked like maple syrup.

Oscar huffed.

The women spoke more about the subject, Mama dismissing the gift as nothing important. Babka holding to her point that every gift a man gave a woman was important. The gift should be returned the next time they went to the mercantile. The German might want to court her, Babka warned.

His mother murmured a few faint words of protest. Suddenly, her voice became livelier, however, when she recalled Mr. Bailey's comment about the subject of returning a gift. She spoke a little more loudly. It was bad manners to return a gift. Mr. Bailey said as much over dinner when the discussion had begun. On this, Babka had no reply, a rare occurrence.

Oscar had to admit he felt grateful Mr. Bailey had come to the ranch despite some of the marks against him. He was a good man, but he'd done some things that troubled Oscar. First, he'd been friendly with Mr. Weber. Then he'd teased Susanna. And finally, he'd very nearly made an enemy of Babka when he thanked her for the dinner that evening, a special roast they called *moravsky vrabec*.

He'd eaten a third helping, earning him a nod of approval from Babka, but then he'd complimented her on the meal.

Those enchiladas really hit the spot...

Babka's jaw had dropped. The room went quiet. Mama's eyes grew big as plums and she hid her smile behind her hand.

Thankfully, Mr. Bailey changed the subject. He started talking about finding Mr. Anderson's donkeys. He had a plan and felt sure the donkeys would be back on the ranch within a week. Susanna's eyes had welled with tears of happiness. And even Babka was smiling at him.

Downstairs, Babka and Mama stopped arguing. For now. Oscar knew the discussion wasn't over. Tomorrow, by breakfast, the two women would pick up where they'd left off.

Oscar closed his eyes and sank into his pillow. He tried not to think about the donkeys, or about the morning he'd found them gone. Mr. Anderson would have been disappointed in Oscar to know the donkeys had been taken two days after he passed.

He pushed the thoughts away with the desperate hope Mr. Bailey would find them and bring them home. The man was big and strong and carried a gun. If Mr. Bailey couldn't find the donkeys, no one could. Oscar dozed off but woke a short time later. The house was dark. A half-moon hung in the sky outside his window.

A sound greeted his ears. A whimper. He sat bolt upright in bed. Another, longer whimper. Oscar threw off the blankets and went down the ladder. Everything was quiet. His mother and grandmother slept. He crept to the door, slipped on his boots, and went outside.

The whimper sounded once more. He hurried to the corner of the house. Oscar looked around, scanning the area. Footsteps broke the stillness of the night.

Beau appeared, still dressed. "What's the trouble, son?"

"I heard a sound. An animal, I think."

When Beau came to his side, he pointed to something moving in the shadows. "Look over there. Lying against the side of the house by the back step."

Oscar marveled at how quickly Beau had spied the source of the noise. He hadn't seen anything until Beau pointed it out.

119

Maybe Rangers were trained in these things. They moved closer. A thumping sound was followed by another pitiful cry.

"It's a dog," Beau said quietly. "He's tied to the step."

Oscar opened his mouth to speak but stood rooted to the spot, unable to find a response. Feeling foolish, he snapped his mouth shut. The dog wriggled and pulled against the rope.

Beau crouched to untie the dog. After a moment of fumbling with the rope and the squirming dog, he managed to loosen the knot and free the animal. The dog, a youngster, whined and jumped and ran circles around them, dashing madly back and forth.

"Does this dog belong to you?" Beau asked.

Oscar shook his head. He lowered and held out his hands. At first the dog didn't notice. He was too busy sniffing a bush. When he saw the boy, he darted towards him, almost knocking him over.

"Is he not yours?" Beau asked once more.

"No, sir. My grandmother won't let me have a dog." He stroked the dog's head. It seemed to relish the attention. He sat very still as Oscar ran his hand the length of his sleek back.

"Why can't you have a dog?"

"Babka's afraid of dogs. She got bitten when she was a girl."

The dog's coat felt soft as down under his palm. The pup gazed at him. The look in the dog's eyes didn't seem like that of a mere puppy. He had deep, longing, soulful eyes. Like a hound dog, Oscar's favorite kind of dog.

Oscar explained more of their family's situation. "We have always moved around a lot. My mom or grandmother would find work as a cook or housekeeper. Even if my grandmother had allowed it, we never had a good place for a dog."

"That's how it was for me too," Beau said.

Oscar looked up with surprise.

Beau shrugged. "My father died when I was a boy. I ended up living with family here and there. Never in one place for too long."

"Your father died?" Oscar could hardly imagine Beau as a boy, much less as a fatherless boy just like him.

"When I was seven."

"And your mother?"

"She passed right after I was born."

Beau spoke matter-of-factly. Oscar could hardly imagine losing both parents.

The dog darted away. Oscar drew a sharp breath, wondering if the dog might vanish into the night.

A woman's voice came from the shadows. "Why, hello there."

Susanna emerged from the darkness with the dog at her side. She crossed the barnyard, the moonlight casting a soft glow across her. She wore a smile. Ever since Beau had promised to help find the donkeys, she'd been happier. Relieved.

"Are we having a meeting?" she asked, sounding amused.

"We found a dog," Beau said in a low voice. "Someone left it tied to the step."

"My word." She stepped closer. "Oh, but he's a little darling."

Oscar felt self-conscious. He tried not to think about his attire. He wore a long nightshirt that didn't even reach the top of his boots. Hopefully, Susanna wouldn't notice his knobby knees.

Susanna's hair hung past her shoulders. Oscar thought she looked sort of nice in the moonlight with her hair down. Most ladies looked special when they wore their hair loose.

She wore the same dress but somehow looked different than when she'd first arrived.

Maybe because Beau was going to help with the donkeys. Or maybe because she was smiling at the dog. The happy expression changed everything about her. When she first came and found out about Mr. Anderson, she looked scared. Like she wanted to cry. Oscar wanted to cry about Mr. Anderson too.

He understood. Still, it was sort of nice to see the happy look on her face. It was good she had some happiness on her first day there. The dog had made her smile, which made Oscar like her even more. Lots of people had animals they especially liked. His mother liked cats. Babka loved horses and donkeys. Oscar liked dogs and it looked like Susanna did too.

The dog nudged Oscar's hand. A request for attention. Oscar smiled and resumed petting the dog.

"Who would do such a thing to a puppy?" Susanna asked.

The moonlight shone on the dog's coat. The color was especially pretty. It was copper. Like Mr. Weber's dog, Sadie. In fact, it was the exact same color...

Oscar drew his hand back from the dog and got to his feet. Slowly, the realization dawned on him. This dog must be Sadie's pup. He recalled Mr. Weber's words that afternoon.

I think what you need here is a good dog, heh? A hound that will let you know a stranger has arrived.

Mr. Weber had left the dog. He'd practically admitted as much to Oscar. He'd probably left the dog just before he and Beau had seen him that afternoon.

An owl hooted on a nearby tree. The dog raced across the yard, barking and fussing. He came to a stop at the bottom of the tree and barked like he wanted to take on the owl. The dog sounded fierce, almost. His bark warbled between a puppy bark and the bark of a grown dog. After a moment of carrying on, the dog tipped his chin to the sky and howled.

Susanna and Beau chuckled.

Oscar shook his head. If this dog hadn't come from Mr. Weber, he might have found the sight comical, but now all he felt was a deep well of disappointment.

He glanced over his shoulder, checking the front door of the house. Any moment Mama and Babka would come out. He'd be in trouble for leaving the house in the middle of the night, and, even worse, they'd see the dog and fuss.

"I don't know where he came from," Beau said. "But I think he's decided this is his new home. He's going to protect it from intruders. Not a bad dog to have around."

The owl, perched high above the dog, spread its wings, and flapped a time or two as if to warn the little dog away. The tactic worked. With a yelp, the dog raced straight back to Oscar. He sat on his haunches at the boy's feet and barked, this time sounding a little less sure of himself.

"I've never had a dog," Susanna mused. "I was sitting at the dining table writing Henry when I heard a bark. I didn't recall seeing a dog today. Mr. Anderson didn't mention one in his ledger. I wondered if I was dreaming."

"Who's Henry?" Beau asked.

The owl flew from the tree, silent as a ghost.

"What a majestic bird. I've never seen an owl before. Your little dog probably thinks he frightened the big frightening creature away," Susanna said. "He's going to think he's quite the brave little guardian!"

"He's not my dog," Oscar said. "I don't know who he belongs to but he's not mine."

"He seems to think you belong to him," Susanna said, gesturing to the dog as he sat at Oscar's feet.

"Who's Henry?" Beau asked again, this time with a little more impatience.

"He's my butler," Susanna said.

"You have a butler?" Oscar asked, trying to ignore the dog. "I've never met anyone who had a butler."

"And I've never met anyone who *didn't* have a butler," Susanna said, teasing gently.

Despite his deep disappointment, Oscar felt a glimmer of happiness as he noted her lightheartedness. Her contentment warmed his heart. It was as if Susanna wasn't going to let anything trouble her if Beau was going to find the donkeys.

She went on, speaking in an animated tone. "I'm writing him in hopes he'll come to Texas." She looked overhead and all around, her expression filled with awe. "I've never seen such a sky, so many stars, such wide-open spaces. I've never *heard* the hoot of an owl. Texas is so beautiful!"

"You don't need a butler," Beau snapped. "What's he going to do? Polish the silver? You need a foreman."

"I don't need either a butler or a foreman." Susanna didn't seem to notice his harsh tone and replied in a cheerful voice. "I have Mr. Anderson's ledger with all the information about the ranch. What more do I need?"

Without waiting for a reply, she went on, "I want Henry to come because the northern winters makes his bones ache. He worked for my mother's family when she was a just a child. He worked for mine ever since I can remember. He needs a warm climate and deserves a comfortable retirement. The poor, dear man. I know he will love Texas. I'm sure of it. He reads a lot of books about cowboys."

Beau nodded. "Your butler reads books about cowboys, does he?"

Susanna didn't answer immediately. She seemed to mull over his question for some reason, like it was a trick question. Oscar wasn't sure what the fuss was about, but knew enough to keep out of it.

"Henry reads a lot of books." She spoke slowly, picking her words with care. "And while I haven't personally seen him read the books, I have it from a good source that he especially likes cowboy stories."

Beau lifted his gaze and let out a long, exasperated sigh. Turning away, he walked a few steps, rubbing his forehead. He muttered under his breath and shook his head. Susanna gave Oscar a questioning look. Oscar shrugged. After a moment of grumbling to himself, Beau ambled back. He said nothing, however, leaving Susanna with a slightly bewildered look on her face.

The owl hooted from a distant tree. A breeze stirred. No one spoke.

The dog yawned and settled onto his belly, keeping part of his weight on Oscar's boots as if reassuring himself the owl wouldn't snatch him while he slept.

Oscar shifted his weight with a growing restlessness. Part of him wanted to stay and talk with Susanna and Beau. He liked them both, and he had to admit he liked how the little dog slept at his feet, but if Babka noticed his bed empty, she'd be sick with worry. He needed to slip back into his house, preferably without anyone noticing.

"What are we going to do with this dog?" he asked, breaking the silence.

"I'll take him for tonight," Beau said. "I have a little dried jerky if he's hungry. In the morning we'll give him proper food."

"He needs a name," Susanna said, brightening.

Oscar looked at the dog with dismay. If they named the dog, it might mean it was staying. He didn't dare hope the dog would stay. Somehow Babka would get her way, like she always did. He sighed wistfully at the little dog sleeping soundly, his head resting on Oscar's boot.

Susanna went on. "We can't keep calling him 'the dog'. Why, even the donkeys have fine names. This little fellow needs a name too. Something brave. Something heroic! Like Lancelot or Galahad."

Beau didn't reply. The deep etch of his scowl showed that he liked her names for the dog about as much as he liked her butler coming to Texas.

Susanna tapped the side of her head. "I'll give it some thought."

Oscar nodded in agreement, because he wanted to think about the dog staying on the ranch and he tried to avoid arguing with ladies.

"I'll sleep on it," Susanna said. "Perhaps inspiration will strike by breakfast."

Beau grumbled something indistinct.

They said good night, each turning to their respective homes. The dog didn't want to go with Beau, however. He wanted to stay with Oscar, which made the boy feel both happy but also a little mad. Darned dog. Babka was going to fuss about having a dog around, especially if it always wanted to be with him. She'd make sure it didn't stay long. He watched with an ache in his heart as Beau scooped the pup in his arms and disappeared into the darkness.

Oscar hurried to his house and slipped inside.

Chapter Fifteen

Susanna

In the predawn darkness, Susanna awoke. Perhaps it was the unfamiliar bed, or the different sounds. She resolved to make use of the time, however, and start her day early. She said her morning prayers, making certain to give thanks for the blessings of her new home in Texas.

After she washed and dressed, she lit the lamp in the small room that Robert must have used for his study. She read the mail that had accumulated on his desk. The first note she saw was one she'd sent him. She read the words she'd written. It seemed like a lifetime ago.

She'd written about signing the proxy and her intention to come to Texas as soon as she was able. And then she'd penned several lines, promising to care for all he held dear.

I look forward to meeting you and learning more of the ranch. I've never cared for anything, but vow to do my best...

Mixed feelings swirled inside her heart. Up until that moment, she didn't know for certain he'd received her note. Now she knew that he'd gotten the note and had read her words about caring for his animals and property.

He'd left her various notes, starting when he'd received a telegraph from the matchmaking agency about her acceptance of his proposal. After that, he wrote more instructions about the property.

Robert Anderson must have sensed he didn't have long.

There wasn't any self-pity in his notes, however. He was matter-of-fact about what needed to be done. He wrote at length about the peach orchard (only plant Early Crawford). The topic of selling hay to Mr. Jahns, the neighbor (a poor idea). A note recommending that she keep a wary eye for his nephew (who'd been nothing but trouble).

The deed to the land has been put in your name. He can't take the ranch. Not legally. But he might try. You never know with that one.

In his last note, he wrote about the Novaks. He'd intended to set aside some money for Oscar's schooling. Victoria wouldn't allow it. He hoped Susanna would have it in her heart to give the boy whatever she could spare when the time came.

Susanna smiled as she imagined helping young Oscar. She could tell from looking at the bank statements, there was more than enough to support the boy. Mr. Anderson had left her a considerable fortune. She noted the figures with mixed feelings, mostly a heavy feeling of responsibility to do right by Mr. Anderson.

Oscar had made a favorable impression from the start. The boy had loved Mr. Anderson and it seemed fitting that she'd help him with his schooling. The rest of the final note was a colorful description of Victoria Novak's impossible, stubborn ways. Robert had a few words about the younger Novak woman as well.

Elsa Novak is as kind as the day is long, but don't be fooled. She's every bit as hardheaded as her mother-in-law. I feel for the boy having to live with those two obstinate females!

Susanna smiled at his words. The man had spent his life alone. Even from his letters, it was clear Robert Anderson was set in his ways. He might have thought the Novak ladies were obstinate, but Susanna felt lucky they lived nearby. She couldn't imagine living on the Anderson ranch all alone.

He'd made some notes about paying the Novaks for their help in the past. There was no indication of recent payments, however. She'd soon remedy that too. The money and the ranch were both a blessing and a responsibility. A promise she'd made and intended to keep.

As she read the other notes on Robert's desk, the dawn brightened the room. She turned down the lamp as the sun crested the horizon. A short time later, Victoria stopped by the house to bring a pot of tea and breakfast.

"I don't know what I'd do without you," Susanna said.

Victoria waved a dismissive hand. "I take care of Robert. Now I take care of you too. I bring a nice lunch for our trip."

Midmorning, Beau brought the buckboard to the house. Susanna stepped out of her front door and paused to put on a sunbonnet.

To her surprise, all three Novaks sat in the back of the wagon. The women were dressed in the same somber dresses as yesterday. They wore dark, matching bonnets. Oscar sat beside his mother dressed in trousers, a shirt and tie.

It was as if the family intended to go to church that morning. Which might have been the case, if it had been the second Sunday when they attended services, according to Robert's ledger. Susanna reminded herself that it was Saturday, however. Her attention drifted to where the little dog sat between Oscar and the front seat. Susanna wondered if Victoria could see the extra passenger from where she sat.

The conversation revolved around not the little dog but something far different. Beau and Victoria debated his attire.

"What's wrong with my shirt?" Beau asked Victoria.

Victoria looked at him primly, a basket on her lap. "It's fine. No problems."

Beau looked bewildered. He muttered a greeting to Susanna and helped her onto the buckboard. Climbing up to sit beside her, he grumbled, "Victoria asked me if she could take my shirt. But won't tell me why. Can't figure why she'd want it. She said she only wanted it for a few minutes."

"You told her no?" Susanna asked.

"Course I did. It's time to go. I don't have time for whatever she had in mind. Who asks a man for his shirt when he's fixing to go to town?"

He snapped the reins, putting the horses into a trot.

His shoulder brushed hers, sending a shiver of awareness across her skin. He looked handsome in his shirt, she had to admit, if only to herself. She eyed the rumpled collar and creased sleeve. Glancing over her shoulder, she found Elsa smiling at her. Elsa moved her hand back and forth as if ironing.

Susanna suppressed a smile and turned back to face forward.

"I didn't even know they were coming," Beau grumbled. "Did you agree to this?"

"Well, not really. She didn't ask if she could."

"She didn't ask me either. I would have told her no. I drove up, stopped the wagon and next thing I know, all three Novaks are climbing into the buckboard. And right off, before I can get a word in edgewise, Victoria is bellyaching about the dog. I told her the dog's mine. End of story. She's quiet one whole minute and then she starts in on my shirt for some reason."

"If it's any consolation, I think she brought a picnic."

"A picnic?" His brows lifted.

"She told me she intended to pack a lunch. I imagine that's what she has in her basket."

He glanced back and heaved a weary sigh. "I prefer to work alone."

"You have to admit she's a good cook."

Beau didn't reply. He kept his attention on the road and driving the team of horses.

"You have to eat," she said, unable to resist teasing him. "Even Rangers need to stop for lunch, don't they?"

He gave Susanna a sheepish smile. "I suppose I can make an exception."

They drove through the Anderson ranch, passing the peach orchards and the pastures. The drive to Sweet Willow was quiet, without any other wagons or riders, but the town itself was a hive of activity. There were few women, she noticed. For every female, there seemed to be twenty cowboys.

Dressed in leather chaps, they rode past, tipping their hats at Susanna and the others. Other cowboys stood outside the barber shop, lined up waiting for a haircut and shave. A saloon stood on the corner. Inside, someone played the piano. A cowboy pushed through the doors and watched them pass, staring unabashedly as if she and the rest of her group were a novelty.

She wondered with some nervousness if Jack Anderson was in Sweet Willow. She wanted to ask Beau if he had any thoughts on the matter. She fretted. If she were to broach the subject, he'd likely use it as an excuse to demand she hire a foreman.

She asked him to stop at the post office, intending to mail Henry's letter and two other letters she'd written that morning. Oscar took the letters for her, along with a few coins and mailed them for her.

131

"Who else are you writing?" Beau asked as they drove to the auction barn. "More servants in Albany?"

"No. Just Henry. The other letters are the two farmers who want to lease the pastures. They'd written Robert to ask if they could graze their cattle in the winter. Both men wanted to lease the entire hundred and fifty acres."

Beau arched a brow. "What did you tell them?"

"I explained I had interest from other farmers. The price had gone up and they should let me know by November first if they wanted to lease the land."

"Look at you," Beau marveled.

A comment from the passengers in the back drew Susanna's attention. Oscar smiled at her. "My grandmother says you're a smart lady. She wants to know if you have Czech heritage?"

Victoria looked at her approvingly and tapped her forehead. "Smart and tough. Like a Czech woman."

Susanna smiled. No one had ever called her tough, and she wasn't entirely sure it was true, but maybe she had changed. If so, it was because she'd come to Texas. She felt a debt of obligation to Robert Anderson and that sense of duty made her brave.

If she could be courageous, she could find the donkeys, care for the property, and do other worthy things like help young Oscar with his studies. Perhaps it was easier to be brave when having courage meant helping others.

They drove to the Bailey Auction Barn. While Beau hitched the team, Victoria had more to say. This time it wasn't about Susanna's business skills or Beau's rumpled shirt.

She pointed to the sign that read *Bailey Auction House.* "This man, Noah Bailey, cares for six children." She knit her brow, trying to think of the right word.

Unable to find the word she was looking for, Victoria turned to Oscar and spoke in Czech. Oscar nodded. "My grandmother is trying to say the children were orphans when Mr. Bailey took them in."

"Noah and Seth are both fine men," Beau said. "After my father died, their family was always good to me. I used to spend summers with them."

The little dog trotted next to Oscar. The boy acted as though he didn't notice a thing while the little dog glanced up as if waiting for a greeting. Victoria frowned at the dog several times, clearly displeased that it was tagging along.

The auction yard was quiet. Beau talked about the crowds that flocked to the auctions, coming from far away to bid on livestock. They walked past the empty barns to the farmyard in the back. Susanna prayed that whoever had bought the little donkeys didn't live too far away. And that they'd agree to sell the donkeys back to her.

Several boys worked in the farmyard, watering animals, grooming horses, and pushing wheelbarrows heaped with hay.

The tallest of the boys jogged over to say hello. He took off his hat and shook hands with Beau.

"This is Holden Bailey," Beau said to Susanna and the others. "My nephew."

The boy, a slim, solemn young man said a friendly hello to the adults and grinned at Oscar. The two boys knew each other from school. Susanna couldn't help comparing the two boys. Holden had spent the morning hard at work. His dusty clothes showed evidence of his labor. Oscar looked neat and tidy but uncomfortable as if he'd rather be hauling water and pushing a barrow.

"You just missed Noah and Sarah," Holden said. "They left to visit her sister."

"That's all right. Maybe you can help us."

"Yessir, I'll do my best."

Beau asked about the donkeys, explaining they'd belonged to Robert Anderson.

Holden brightened. "I know where two of them are. Me and my brothers bought the one with the white spot on his face."

"That's Michael," Oscar said.

"Is he here?" Susanna asked, too excited to contain herself.

"Yes, ma'am. In the barn."

"Oh, my, can we see him?" she asked.

Holden took them to the barn and took them inside. The scent of hay wafted through the air. Horses came to the doors of their stalls to gaze at the group of visitors. Holden led them to a stall in the back, away from the other animals.

A horse stood on one side of the stall. A few paces away, a donkey dozed in the hay, as pretty as a picture. Susanna's breath caught in her throat. She hadn't dared hope they would find one of the donkeys so quickly. He was the dearest little creature she'd ever seen. He stirred and opened his eyes, blinking a few times. It was clear that Michael was unimpressed with his audience because he promptly went back to sleep.

Victoria murmured a few words in her native tongue. She rummaged in the basket and took out a small parcel. Handing the basket to Oscar, she called softly to the donkey. Michael opened his eyes again. When he saw Victoria at the door, he got up from the hay.

Victoria chuckled as she unwrapped the linen covering. "Michael loves apples. I cut into pieces because he is too small to eat the apple."

Susanna smiled as the donkey sniffed the apple slice. "What a little sweetheart."

Oscar agreed. "He's the nicest one of the group."

Victoria protested good-naturedly as she fed the donkey an apple slice. "All are sweet. All are little angels."

Holden added his own opinion. "He's made a big difference for my mare. When Tilly lost her foal, she stopped eating. I worried I might lose her too, but Michael keeps her company and she's not so lonesome. I had to use every bit of my savings to buy him, but it was worth every penny to help Tilly."

The horse whickered when she saw the apples. She came to the door and Victoria gave her a slice too. The horse sniffed the linen eagerly which prompted Victoria to give her another slice. Victoria stroked the horse's forehead, offering soft words of comfort.

Beau told Holden that the donkeys hadn't belonged to the man who had sold them. The boy's eyes widened with alarm. His face reddened.

"We didn't know about any of that. Uncle Seth bought one too. Francine took one look at the donkeys and begged him to buy one for her."

Susanna asked, "I wonder if you would consider selling this little fellow back to me. Perhaps when Tilly's recovered from losing her foal."

Holden nodded slowly. Susanna suspected he was agreeing to be polite. She felt a pang of guilt for asking the boy to part with the donkey. What if he'd become attached?

"I promised Mr. Anderson I'd take care of his donkeys," she explained. "If you sell Michael back to me when you're done, I'll pay you double what you paid."

Holden's brows lifted. A smile tugged at the corners of his mouth. "Double?"

"Yes. And if you ever need a companion for an ailing mare, I'll let you borrow Michael."

After that, the deal was as good as done.

Holden and Susanna shook hands. All three Novaks smiled and thanked Holden. Susanna's fretfulness eased somewhat. While she had one donkey, and knew the whereabouts of the other, she still didn't have them on the Anderson ranch. When she got them all back home, she would have done her duty. Until then, she wouldn't feel entirely at ease.

They lingered by the stall a little longer before leaving the barn.

Holden walked them back to the buckboard. The little dog was never more than a few paces from the group. Susanna noticed Oscar keeping an eye on the pup just in case it got into mischief.

Susanna and Holden talked about the other donkeys. He promised to ask his father to search the sales ledger to find out who had bought Rafael. When they got to the buckboard, Holden hinted that it might be difficult getting Gabriel back from the other family.

"Francine loves her donkey. She grooms him all the time and tries to get him to wear hats which he hates. She says she wants to train him to pull a cart. She might not be willing to sell Gabriel." Holden glanced at Oscar. "And she can be stubborn, right, Oscar?"

Oscar nodded. "She's a tough girl. The toughest at school."

"That might well be," Susanna said. "But it so happens that just this morning, Mrs. Novak said she thinks I'm tough. We'll see if I can't win Francine over."

Holden nodded but didn't look entirely convinced. "Yes, ma'am."

Chapter Sixteen

Beau

They left the town of Sweet Willow, taking the road back to the Anderson ranch. The winding road ran along the same stream that edged Susanna's property, a cheerful little brook lined with immense cypress trees. They grew along the bank, their limbs stretching across the water.

Beau glanced at Susanna as she rode in silence beside him. Instead of looking happy about finding a donkey, maybe two, she looked worried. He noted the tension around her pretty eyes. She didn't give in to her usual easy, sassy smile. Instead, she seemed lost in her thoughts.

Babka asked about finding a pretty spot to picnic. Beau agreed and stopped the buckboard near the stream, in the shade of one of the cypress trees.

The pup jumped down and raced joyfully to the water's edge, stopping at the bank, his brow wrinkled with concern. He barked a time or two and ran back to Oscar. Beau thought the little dog seemed awful fond of a boy determined to ignore him.

Beau helped the ladies down from the wagon. When he set his hands around Susanna's waist, he felt the urge to hold her a little longer than needed. He wondered if she felt the same way when he heard the catch in her breath.

The Novaks went to the riverbank and set out a blanket.

Beau wanted to linger a moment with Susanna. They'd hardly been alone since coming to the ranch. One or all three of the Novaks had been nearby much of the time.

"I'll take you to my cousin's house tomorrow," he said quietly. "Hopefully, Noah will get word to us about the third donkey."

"Rafael," Susanna said. "I'm very grateful for all your help, Beau."

"You don't look grateful, not that you need to. But I'd like to help with whatever you're fretting about."

"At first, I felt terrible asking to buy the donkey from the boy. And then I felt badly that I was spending Robert's money so freely."

"It's your money now, sweetheart. Besides, you're fixing to make a lot more when you lease the pastures."

She looked past him to the river and let out a sigh. "It seems odd to spend another person's money."

Beau shrugged. "What's Robert going to do with it? He can't spend it now, can he?"

"No, he can't."

"You did a good thing today. You're getting your donkey back and Holden's made a little money."

She nodded. "I suppose you're right. I don't know why it feels strange to spend money. Maybe because I've always had to ask for everything. Mostly, I want to do the right thing. I feel a responsibility to keep my promise. To be a good caretaker."

The soft, gentle tone of her voice stirred something inside him. He lifted his hand, cupped her jaw, and stroked her cheek with his thumb. She gazed at him with surprise. He half-expected her to retreat. Instead, she smiled at him.

"Thank you," she said softly. "For everything."

"I'm happy to help. That's what Rangers do. It's our job."

She looked a little dismayed by his response. "Your duty?"

"That's right. That's why I'm here." Her skin felt soft as silk beneath his thumb. He wished he could pull her closer and brush a kiss across her lips.

"To serve and protect," he added.

Her eyes filled with a soft look. She parted her lips as if she wanted to respond, but a sound interrupted them.

An approaching wagon put an end to the sweet moment. Reluctantly, he dropped his hand and moved away, circling the wagon to see who approached.

Mr. Weber drove the wagon from the mercantile. When he saw Beau, he waved.

"Tell Victoria I'll be down in a moment," Beau said to Susanna as she made her way to the riverbank.

Mr. Weber stopped his team of mules. "Mr. Bailey, everything all right, I hope."

"Just fine. We're coming from town. The ladies wanted to stop for a picnic."

Mr. Weber glanced at the women, letting his gaze linger a moment before turning his attention back to Beau. "You will be returning to your duties soon?"

Beau wondered why the man would ask such a question. "Soon enough."

"It's a fine thing you're doing. Staying on the ranch to help Mrs. Anderson. I'm glad there's a man on the property." He glanced at the river once again, pursing his lips.

The man didn't look glad at all.

"I'm happy to do it," Beau replied.

It occurred to him that he was, in fact, happy to stay at the ranch. A strange notion. Usually, he lived his life in the saddle, always on the move. Always thinking about his work, protecting civilians. He hadn't thought about that much lately.

Or adding to his list of the criminals he'd caught. He still wanted to protect people, but now had a specific person in mind. Susanna Anderson.

"Jack Anderson is no good," Mr. Weber said, his eyes darkening. "If he comes back, he will cause problems for the women. I will find a foreman for Mrs. Anderson. Before you leave, I hope."

Beau nodded. He'd forgotten about talking to Mr. Weber about a foreman. Of course, Susanna needed help. He reminded himself the foreman had been his idea all along.

"I have two young men who would be fine foremen," Mr. Weber said. "Very good men. Strong. Hard-working."

"Sounds about right," Beau said the words because they seemed the thing to say.

"I will send them to meet with Mrs. Anderson very soon." Mr. Weber spoke with pride in his voice. "I have known Hans Oltorf and Siegfried Schmidt since they were young boys. They are good workers. Strong."

A spark of irritation flickered inside Beau's thoughts. "Right. Strong, so you said."

The sound of Susanna's voice floated on the breeze. She called to the dog and laughed when he bounded along the water's edge. Her laughter loosened a tight spot inside him. Despite that, or maybe because of the feeling, he noted a sense of annoyance with Mr. Weber's news.

He pictured a couple of young bucks strolling up to Susanna's front door. Up until that point, he'd felt strongly Susanna needed a foreman. Oscar was a good boy, hard-working and kind-hearted, but he was still a boy. He needed to go to school and work on his studies. Susanna needed a man to help her with the animals and the land.

Mr. Weber went on. "Mrs. Anderson will like one of them, yes?"

"Maybe."

Mr. Weber glanced over his shoulder to study the spot on the bank where Susanna sat with the Novaks. He frowned. "I thought you wished for her to have help. I must say, I don't like the idea of the women living there all alone. They need a man's help. Especially at night."

Beau winced. Especially at night. Well, of course the women needed help at night. Which would mean the young man would live in the cabin where he now stayed, the cabin that was just a few paces from Susanna's.

He took off his hat and raked his fingers through his hair before putting it back on.

"Of course. Before you send them, let me discuss the matter with Susanna, one on one. I think I should convince her that she needs help on the ranch before a couple of boys come knocking on her door offering to be her foreman."

"Hans and Siegfried are not boys, Mr. Bailey. They are young men who are in their early twenties, maybe even older than Mrs. Anderson."

"Fine," Beau snapped. "I still want to talk to her first."

Mr. Weber smiled. "Very well. Just so we have this worked out before you leave. I will check with you in a few days. I am concerned for Mrs. Anderson, but also for the Novaks. I'm sure you understand."

"Yes, of course. I won't leave unless there is a man to take care of the ranch."

Mr. Weber seemed satisfied with that.

"Thank you, Beau. I hope you enjoy your picnic. I see you brought your little dog, heh? Very nice. He will like the water." He nodded a polite farewell and was on his way.

Beau joined the group at the riverbank. Oscar and the three ladies sat on a blanket in the dappled shade of the cypress. The stream flowed behind them, offering a restful scene. Victoria had unpacked her basket. The savory aroma made his stomach rumble.

He'd shared a number of meals with Susanna and the Novaks over the past few days. He'd gotten spoiled, both by the good food and the fine company. Taking a spot across from Susanna, he sat with his back to the immense tree where he could take in the serene beauty of the setting as well as steal an admiring look at Susanna when he got the chance.

Victoria sat by the basket serving food as she chattered about the donkeys and how much she missed them. Elsa added her own thoughts about the animals, wondering if they missed each other. The three were always together and likely felt lonesome for one another.

Susanna regarded him with curiosity, probably wondering about what he'd discussed with Mr. Weber. Her smile was warm and her gaze lingered. A sort of silent communication passed between them, or so it seemed to Beau.

Victoria Novak, on the other hand, was impatient to learn all about Mr. Weber. When Beau was settled, she turned to the topic of the man's visit. "What did the German want?"

"He's looking for a foreman for Susanna."

Her brows lifted. Her expressions softened. "I see. That's nice."

"He's got a couple of German fellows he thinks are good workers."

Beau didn't include Mr. Weber's plans to bring the men out to the ranch soon, maybe even that evening. It was something he'd rather not think about just yet. He watched Victoria as the hard look returned to her eyes. She didn't care for the idea at all, which showed in the way she served the food. She jabbed a potato dish with her serving spoon and dropped the food on the plate like she blamed the potatoes.

Elsa shook her head and sighed, taking a plate from Victoria and passing it to Beau. "Victoria doesn't like Germans."

He accepted the food as he suppressed a smile. "What do you have against Germans?"

Victoria lifted her chin, her eyes flashed with displeasure. "A German man stole from my family."

Beau frowned.

Elsa spoke softly. "Not this again."

"He was a very bad man." Victoria waved her serving spoon in the air for emphasis. "My family was hungry. He stole a big basket of carrots."

Victoria went on, her voice growing more vehement as she told the story. "It was winter. My family needed the food. The German man didn't care. The door to the house was open. He came in and take the carrots."

The little dog trotted over to the party and lay beside Oscar. The boy listened to his grandmother. He was so absorbed in Victoria's tale, he didn't seem to notice he'd started to pet the dog on the head.

"That's just the sort of thing a Texas Ranger could help you with," Beau said. "Did you report the theft?"

Susanna smiled at him. He was trying his best to be cordial to Victoria and was pleased Susanna noticed. He winked in return. Oscar looked impressed as if he hadn't imagined that the Texas Rangers helped with that sort of trouble.

"In the beginning," Beau said. "The Rangers were formed to protect the borders. Nowadays we go after all sorts of criminals. Even carrot thieves."

Victoria pursed her lips as if she thought he was teasing her.

"It's the truth. I've even caught a few thieves myself."

Elsa laughed. "This didn't happen in Texas."

"Where did it happen?"

"In the old country," Elsa said, her eyes twinkling. "Almost a hundred years ago."

"A hundred years ago!" Beau exclaimed.

Victoria gave him a severe look, daring him to smile.

Beau considered how much he liked Mrs. Novak's cooking. Offending the lady seemed like a very bad idea and he resolved to choose his words carefully.

"Well, I'd like to think I'm a pretty good Ranger. I've chased after thieves that stole cattle, mules, payroll off stagecoaches and even one desperado who stole a crate of Bibles, if you can imagine such a thing. I'm happy to go where I'm needed. But I don't suppose I can offer much help in the case of carrots stolen a century ago."

Victoria grumbled a response Beau didn't understand.

Oscar translated. "She says it's too bad there weren't Texas Rangers in Czechoslovakia and thank you anyway."

"Yes, ma'am."

When Victoria finished serving the food, Beau offered a prayer of thanksgiving. A rush of warmth came over him. He was accustomed to time alone and usually craved solitude. But sitting with Susanna and the Novaks, he noted a contentment he'd never known.

They ate their lunch on the side of the stream, enjoying the fine afternoon. Beau refused to think about the days slipping away or the young men who would come looking for work on the ranch. He didn't want to think of all the young men who'd very much like to be in his boots at that moment in time.

Chapter Seventeen

Susanna

Over the next few days, Susanna waited for word from Noah Bailey about the third donkey. She also hoped to visit Francine, but the dark skies threatened ominously. Thunder rumbled in the distance. Victoria Novak complained about her wrists. They ached which meant a storm was coming.

Unable to continue her search for the animals, Susanna busied herself with other matters. According to Robert's ledger, the peach orchard produced a bountiful harvest. He sold much of the fruit, but over the past two years, the yield had fallen. She found a book about fruit orchards and studied how to care for the trees.

The trees needed to be trimmed and shaped. If neglected, the trees would produce less fruit over time. Even without the evidence in the ledger, Susanna could plainly see that Robert had not cared for the orchard. She explained her findings to Beau and the Novaks one evening at dinner and spoke of her plans to care for the orchard and restore the plentiful harvest.

Victoria had approved, once again tapping her forehead to show her admiration. Beau had been impressed as well, smiling at her from the other side of the dinner table. His smile made her happier than she would have imagined.

The subject of the donkeys still troubled her. The empty paddock caused her continued distress. On the afternoon of the third day, when Susanna could no longer contain her unease, she sought out Beau. He'd kept busy, working on various projects around the Anderson ranch.

She found him in the shed, sawing a piece of lumber. He stopped when he saw her approach. Setting the saw aside, he smiled and gestured to his work. "I decided I couldn't spend one more night on Will Anderson's bed. Getting tired of my feet hanging off the edge."

"Will and Robert must not have been very tall men. I can scarcely pass under some of the doorways in my house. I'm certain you'd hit your head on most."

"I'll bet you came down here because you're fretting about the donkeys. Don't you worry about Gabriel. Francine might be a tad ornery, but she'll do the right thing. Those animals should never have been sold in the first place."

Susanna felt the heat rise to her cheeks. "You could tell what I was thinking?"

He feigned a look of dismay. "It's a tad worrisome, isn't it?"

"I don't mind, but it might cause you some trouble."

"That so?"

"A big, famous lawman like you, guessing what a woman fretted about?"

He frowned, this time his expression was genuine. "Famous?"

"Elsa said she read about you in the paper. That you'd apprehended three men single-handedly."

He rubbed his jaw and grumbled. He turned his attention to the wood plank he'd been working on and rubbed his thumb along the edge.

"I feel very fortunate that you're here, Beau."

He nodded. "I'm happy to help."

"You're taking time from your work and spending it here when I'm sure there are many other things you could be doing. Spending time with the other Baileys, for instance."

Beau held her gaze. For a long moment, he said nothing. A few days ago, he'd stood close and cupped her jaw. He'd touched her in an intimate way, in broad daylight by the buckboard. His touch had both surprised and thrilled her.

Finally, he spoke, a soft warmth in his gaze. "I'd rather be here with you, Susanna."

His deep voice chased a shiver down her spine.

She yearned to ask him if he'd stay on. Each night, when she said her prayers, she always added a few words of thanks for Beau Bailey. There was no way to ask him if he would remain, however. To ask him to stay with her would start another debate about a foreman. Not only that, but he had his work and a life apart from hers. Very far apart.

Sensing her dismay, he offered a teasing smile and motioned to the wooden bedframe. "Aside from the bed, I can't complain. Victoria Novak's cooking is mighty good. The company is fine. I can't say this time has been too bad. It will be even better tonight when I can stretch out and get a good night's sleep."

"When will you leave?" she asked.

"I should report to Austin in a week."

"Which means you'll have to set out in a few days' time."

He shrugged. "I can make the trip in two days' time."

Her throat felt tight. A chill came over her. She let out a shuddering breath and walked to the doorway of the shed. The dark sky looked even more ominous than it had earlier. The breeze blew cooler and she wondered if the storm might finally break.

"I can stay on, if you like," he said quietly.

"No, I'll have to manage on my own eventually. Fortunately, I have Robert's ledger."

Beau closed the distance between them, stopping behind her. Her breath caught in her throat. Her thoughts returned to the moment he'd touched her a few days before. His touch had caused turmoil in her mind. She realized that now. It had been a mistake.

She turned to face him, determined to keep a distance between them.

"See all that land?" he asked gruffly.

Frowning, she followed his gaze. The wind swept across the fields. The orchards in the distance looked stark against the darkening sky. The view from the shed was beautiful even, with the fearsome clouds gathering.

"I see it," she said. "What about it?"

"It's all yours now. You're managing things, caring for the land even better than Robert Anderson." His smile widened. "Sweetheart, you don't need that ledger."

She wasn't sure what to say. Of course, she needed the ledger. How else would she take care of everything that needed doing?

"You just need a man around to help you carry out your plans."

"A man would just take over. I've spent my life living under my father's thumb. I don't want to depend on a man's help."

"Just because you get a man's help doesn't mean he's going to make your life miserable. What about your friend, Harold?"

"Who?"

"The butler."

"Henry."

"Did you live under his thumb?"

"Of course not. He worked for my family. And...and...he was Henry. A kind person. He took care of me which is why I want to take care of him."

"Right. You take care of each other. That's the way it works. People can be stronger together."

"Fine words from you, *Lieutenant* Bailey."

"Guess I'm working things out too."

Susanna was about to reply with a cutting remark. Before she could speak, thunder rolled across the sky. The sound was closer. Victoria had promised a storm. She'd given a stern warning and the weather probably didn't dare refuse her prediction.

When another blast of thunder rumbled, Susanna resolved to return to the house before it began to rain. She bid Beau goodbye and hurried home. The rain did not come until late that night, however. The heavy downpour came with a vengeance along with thunder that shook the small cabin.

The fury of the storm was unlike anything she'd ever seen before. She had to admit she was alarmed, perhaps even a little frightened. Late in the evening, Beau knocked on the door, drenched from the rain.

"I wanted to check on you before I turned in," he said.

"I'm fine. Thank you." She winced at the tremble in her voice.

If he heard, he gave no sign. His eyes showed concern, not any of his usual teasing expression.

"I could stay if you like, Susanna. If you're troubled by the storm."

"Of course not. I can manage perfectly fine on my own."

He leaned against the doorway, water dripping off the rim of his hat. Behind him, lightning flashed. The jagged streak was so bright, it lit the land and very nearly turned the dark of night to daytime. She fought the urge to tug him inside the house and slam the door behind him. What would Victoria Novak say about that, she wondered. Nothing good, most likely.

"Have you noticed any leaks in the roof?" he asked.

"Not a single drop."

A splashing sound came from the darkness. The dog bounded onto the porch and dashed inside. He left a trail of muddy pawprints, disappearing down the hallway.

Beau didn't move from where he stood. He smiled and shrugged. "I suppose Toby wants to sleep here tonight. He favors a soft blanket under the bed."

"Toby?" Susanna asked, glancing over her shoulder. "You named the dog?"

"'Course I named him. He's a good dog. Maybe a little afraid of thunder, but he'll keep you company through the storm."

"Thank you."

"I'm here to serve and protect." With that, Beau touched the brim of his hat and wished her a good night.

Susanna wasn't entirely sure she wanted the company of a wet, frightened dog. It was too late to argue, however, as Beau had vanished into the darkness. The rain poured off the roof and formed a swift stream along the front of the cabin.

She shut the door, slid the bolt across and went to her room. Toby huddled under the bed with his nose tucked under his tail. She found a worn blanket and made a soft bed for the pup under her own bed.

After her prayers, Susanna slipped beneath the quilt the Novak ladies had made for her. She lay in bed, listening to the storm. The first few nights she'd slept in the cabin, she'd been struck by the quiet. There were various sounds of wind and the owl that liked to hoot outside the window, but the quiet was so different from what she'd known in Albany.

Thunderstorms were different in Texas. They were louder, more violent, far more frightening. The thunder shook the small cabin, rattling the windows with each blast. The little cabin shook around her.

The dog slept quietly under the bed, and she felt comforted by his soft, rhythmic breathing. At times she dozed, only to be awakened by the rumbling sky. Sometime in the wee hours of the morning, she drifted off to fitful dreams.

Chapter Eighteen

Beau

Beau stood by the window watching the storm unleash its fury. The storm didn't bother him, exactly, but he'd seen lightning storms start fires, and he knew firsthand what fires could do.

His worst scars, and the most pain he'd ever felt in his life, came from burns across his face, neck and right shoulder, caused by a blaze in a Waco hotel. He'd saved five people that night, and he was grateful to escape with his own life, but never again would he feel invincible. Even though he'd never admit it, there was one thing that scared him, and that was fire.

The last few days he'd thought of little else than the girl from Albany. Susanna and her donkeys had taken over his mind. He felt restless, knowing that Susanna was alone tonight, during the storm, and might be alone for a long time when he went back to his work. He had to admit a desire to stay close to her, especially when there was trouble around. How could he leave her in a few days' time? He paced the length of the small, cramped cabin.

Finally, unable to think of anything other than Susanna alone in the cabin, he searched the cabin for paper and ink. The one thing that might ease his mind would be staying with Susanna a little longer. He set the lamp on a small table and penned a letter to his commanding officer, requesting more time to take care of some personal matters.

While he wrote, he considered that he hadn't even visited Noah or Seth in the time he'd spent in Sweet Willow. He didn't have much family, and these two men were the closest family he had. He'd been so concerned with Susanna that he had scarcely thought about them. Seth and Noah would likely be amused he'd gotten caught up, fretting about a woman and the plight of a bunch of donkeys.

As he finished the letter, the storm continued. The downpour turned into a drizzle for a short while and back to heavy rain. Lightning flashed, followed by a blast of thunder that shook the rafters.

He prepared to turn in for the night. He might even enjoy a few hours of decent sleep in the new bed. With his letter completed, he resolved to check on Susanna one last time.

When he stepped out the front door, the first thing he noticed was the smell of smoke. Without any conscious thought, he broke into a run. The rain blurred his vision. He stumbled in the mud but managed to regain his footing. Wiping the water from his brow, he splashed across the path. The acrid smell of smoke was stronger. Nothing appeared amiss from the outside. He saw no fire. The sound of flames, however, was unmistakable.

He heard Toby's bark from inside.

When he tried the door, he found it bolted. The heavy barricade would take precious moments to break down. Instead, he kicked the nearby window. It shattered. He climbed through the opening.

"Susanna!"

There was no response. He called again, but only heard the crackle of the fire burning somewhere in the back of the cabin.

Smoke had begun to fill the front of the cabin. It came from the hallway, the direction of the bedrooms. He charged into the dark, choking smoke. An instant later, he banged into a doorway, the impact sending a jolt of pain down his body.

After that, he tried to keep his pace slow and steady. He wouldn't do Susanna any good if he cracked his head and got knocked out. He forced himself to move more slowly, feeling his way down the hallway with outstretched hands.

He coughed. His breath wheezed. Somewhere in the house, the little puppy barked.

Turning toward Toby, he ran his hands along the wall to guide his steps. He made his way, praying he was getting closer to her instead of farther away. He had no idea where he was. He moved blindly.

Desperation mounted.

While he'd been inside Susanna's house several times, he only knew the kitchen and parlor. The back rooms were unknown to him. He didn't want to call her name. He held his breath as much as he could. If he took in too much smoke, it would slow him down even more.

The smoke grew thick. The air felt hotter with every step. The fire snapped and hissed. His eyes burned and teared. Where was Susanna?

Please, God, let me find my girl...

At the end of the hallway, his fingers met a soft, feminine form. His heart quaked. He thanked God to find Susanna slumped against the wall.

She coughed and gasped for air. He lifted her and turned back the way he'd come. A flash of lightning lit the windows, showing him the way. He moved swiftly. When he reached the door, he set her down, keeping a firm grasp around her waist and threw the bolt back.

He strode from the burning cabin. The rain pelted them. Lightning flashed. A crash came from the burning cabin. The blaze roared over the sound of the downpour.

When he got to the door of his cabin, he kicked it open. Susanna held on tightly, her arms looped around his neck. He'd intended to put her down but found he couldn't let go. Instead, he sank to the edge of the bed, keeping her in his arms.

They sat together for some time, how long, Beau wasn't sure.

"Are you alright?" he asked.

"I am."

She sounded weary. Her voice was rough from the smoke. He wrapped her in his blanket and returned to the window. The fire still burned, but the rain and wet grounds would keep it from spreading.

Susanna came to his side and watched the fire. "Thank you for coming for me."

He pulled her back into his arms. "Susanna," he whispered. Cupping her jaw, he lowered his head. "I'll always come for you."

His lips brushed hers.

She murmured with surprise but didn't retreat. "Because it's your duty? To serve and protect?"

Holding her in his arms made him think of a hundred things. His duty to serve and protect didn't play much part in what went through his mind. Instead, he recalled the fear that consumed him when he saw the flames and smoke.

Despite his fears, despite his past, he'd charged into Susanna's house. It was as if he had no choice. The only thing he knew was the deep need to find Susanna and carry her to safety.

There was more to it, however. More than just a need to serve and protect. He couldn't live a life apart from Susanna. He knew that now.

He lowered to kiss her lips. She was surprised at first, judging from the soft, quick breath, but then she kissed him back. The kiss was sweet, tender. He reveled in the feel of her soft lips, her slim frame, so delicate in his embrace.

Later, that night, she fell asleep. He rested beside her, exhausted but awake. Listening to her soft breathing, his heart ached to think of her alone in the cabin, frightened and defenseless. He wanted to wrap her in his arms and never let her go.

Chapter Nineteen

Oscar

After the stormy night, Oscar wanted nothing more than to remain in his bed and sleep. It was a school day, though. He waited for Babka to call upstairs for him to come for breakfast. The noises coming from the kitchen didn't sound like the usual sounds, however.

He sat up in bed and listened more intently. A woman's voice filled the cabin. It was his mother, speaking in a rapid, panicked tone, so quickly that Oscar couldn't make out the words. He was up, out of bed in an instant and clambering down the ladder the next.

Both Mama and Babka were gone, however. The cabin was empty. The front door stood open. He hurried to the porch. The sun had not yet crested the horizon. The soft light of dawn lay over the land. He hurried to the garden. It was quiet, as was the chicken coop. He rushed down the path towards Mr. Anderson's home.

When it came into view, he saw the burning remnants. Stopping in his tracks, he stared. Smoke wafted across the barnyard. The little cabin was no more. A few wooden supports remained, blackened, and burning with the charred remnants of the blaze.

Stunned, he wandered closer. It was gone. All of it. The little porch where he spent long afternoons, talking with Mr.

Anderson, had been reduced to ash. The rest of the house smoldered. The fireplace and chimney jutted into the clear morning sky.

His grandmother's stern voice could be heard from Beau's cabin. Oscar had been so shocked by the sight of the ruined cabin, that he'd forgotten about Susanna and Beau and even the little dog. He hurried to the cabin, running through the mud barefooted, wearing only his nightshirt.

"Come Beau. You must sit up," Babka demanded.

"Please, Beau," his mother added in a gentle voice.

They stood over the bed. Beau lay beside Susanna. He appeared to be sleeping.

Oscar drew closer as he considered the horrifying possibility that the man was dead. And maybe Susanna too. His mind rebelled. He refused to believe the awful notion. He'd lost too many people he cared for and loved. It wasn't possible. He shook his head. No.

Mama grimaced. "He's hurt. So much blood."

"You're right. I thought it was Susanna."

Oscar noted the way Beau held Susanna. His arms were clasped around the woman's waist. In the back of Oscar's mind, he noted the impropriety. Any minute Babka would fuss about Beau touching Susanna in such an unacceptable way. It soon became clear, however, his grandmother was more concerned about the deep cut on Beau's shoulder.

She peered down at the wound and frowned. "You will need stitches, Mr. Bailey."

Oscar was not sure why his grandmother spoke so formally to Beau, but something about her comment got his attention. His eyes opened immediately. He blinked in confusion. Susanna stirred in his arms. When he didn't let go of her, Mama gently coaxed his hands free.

Babka sent Oscar for her sewing basket. He ran back to the house, and without pausing to put on shoes or more clothes, hurried back with her sewing things. By the time he returned, Beau sat on the edge of the bed beside Susanna.

Oscar let out a sigh of relief. He was so grateful. He looked around the cabin, wondering where the little dog was. Beau said he liked to sleep under the bed, but the pup was nowhere to be seen. Oscar waited to ask. At least the dog hadn't been staying in the other cabin, thank goodness.

"What happened?" Mama asked, bringing Susanna a wet rag to wipe the soot from her face.

"I don't know," Susanna said, taking the rag and rubbing her face. The rag only served to spread the dark ash over more of her pale skin. "The storm seemed to be passing. I fell asleep. I don't know how the fire started."

"Lightning strike," Beau muttered. "It had to be."

"Is there anything left?" Susanna asked.

Babka and Mama shared a worried glance.

Susanna's eyes widened. No one spoke for a long moment. Her eyes filled with tears as she shook her head.

"Everything's gone," she said tearfully. "All of Robert's belongings. My clothes. The ledgers he kept so carefully. What will I do without his notes?"

She and Beau sat on the side of the bed. He took the rag from her hand and gently wiped the soot from her face. His efforts proved no better than hers, but that didn't seem to bother him. He carried on, smearing soot a little more evenly across her jaw.

"You'll manage just fine," Beau said. "You're already managing just fine."

Oscar watched Beau's clumsy attempts to clean Susanna's face. The gesture surprised him a little. Beau didn't seem accustomed to gentleness. Susanna hardly seemed to notice since she was too distraught, but she accepted the comfort, leaning a little closer as he tended to her. That was different too, since Beau and Susanna usually argued about everything under the sun, or so it seemed to Oscar.

"The important thing is you're both safe," Babka said, turning to rummage through her sewing basket.

"I can't believe it. Robert's house is gone. I feel just awful. It's like a terrible dream." Susanna stared out the window, dazed. "It's gone."

"Now listen, Susanna," Beau said. "You didn't do anything to cause that fire. It could just as easily have happened to Robert as to you. There's no way you could have prevented a lightning strike."

"You can build new," Babka said.

"You can stay in this cabin," Oscar suggested.

Babka gave him a severe look. "This is Beau's cabin."

"Susanna could marry Beau," Mama pointed out.

Oscar's jaw dropped. Beau marry Susanna? Susanna had already been married. How could she take a second husband? He waited for Babka to voice her extreme disapproval. To his astonishment, his grandmother nodded.

Babka unspooled a length of thread and snipped it off. "I think so too. Beau, you should ask Susanna to marry you."

Beau nodded and muttered a reply but seemed mostly concerned with Babka's activity with the needle and thread.

"Marry?" Susanna asked.

Mama folded her arms across her chest, directing her words to Babka. "Ah, maybe not. If she marries again, she brings dishonor to Robert."

Babka grumbled as she searched for a needle. When she didn't respond with the usual argument, Oscar scratched his head, frowning. Maybe Babka had changed her mind about something. Even Mama looked a little surprised.

"Finally," Babka said, holding up a sharp needle for everyone to see. "I find my best needle."

Beau shook his head. "I hate needles."

The needle flashed in the morning sun. Oscar recoiled. He'd never had stitches before. He felt sorry for Beau. He felt a little sorry for Babka too even though she didn't seem to be troubled by the prospect of stitching Beau's shoulder. If anything, she looked a little pleased.

She hummed as she held the needle to the window and searched for the eye.

"I don't need stitches," Beau argued.

His voice sounded rough, like he had a cold. When he coughed a couple of times, Oscar realized Beau must have taken smoke from the fire last night. Susanna spoke in the same raspy voice. Oscar winced.

"I'm very good at stitches," Babka said as she threaded her needle. "If I'd been born a man, I could study for medicine."

Beau regarded her with growing dismay. He glanced down at his shoulder. It no longer bled, but the gash was deep. Oscar's mother urged him to remove his shirt. He adamantly refused. A heated discussion arose. Babka lapsed into Czech. Mama translated for the most part, but as the argument progressed, she began adding a few native phrases to her English.

Beau glared at both women and shook his head, growing more obstinate with each passing moment.

Finally, Susanna prevailed. She leaned close to him and whispered in his ear, he relented. With a weary sigh, he began to unbutton what was left of his tattered shirt.

"All right," he said reluctantly. "I'll take off my shirt if you insist. But my chest ain't as pretty as the rest of me."

He slipped off his shirt, grimacing in pain, and tossed it aside. Oscar stared in shock at Beau's bare skin. The man's chest was crisscrossed with scars. The three women recoiled at the sight of his scarred neck and shoulder.

Oscar's stomach tightened. He had to avert his gaze. The blood, the scars, the prospect of his grandmother poking Beau with her needle was too much. Spots danced in his vision as he staggered to the doorway.

The cool, morning air helped a little as long as he avoided looking at the burned shell of Mr. Anderson's home. He stood in the doorway, leaning against the frame. Cold sweat beaded on his forehead.

Behind him, the adults carried on, talking about the fire. Oscar felt grateful no one noticed him.

Beau mentioned someone named Toby. Oscar held his midsection, trying to calm his churning stomach. His thoughts swirled. He wondered who Toby was. Perhaps he was a friend of Beau's. He wiped the sleeve of his nightshirt against his clammy forehead.

He was a mess. Muddy. Barefooted. Sick to his stomach.

Distantly, he heard Beau talk more about the fire and how someone named Toby had helped.

"I was walking blind," Beau said. "With the dark and the smoke, I couldn't see my hand in front of my face. With every step, I was praying to God."

Oscar eyed the remnants of the cabin, trying to imagine the blaze. The notion of Mr. Anderson's house in flames made him want to weep. He tried to look away but could not.

Beau went on talking about the fire.

Oscar only half listened. His eyes stung. A tear fell. He swiped it away hastily, chiding himself for crying like a child. He wasn't a child. Even Mr. Anderson had treated him like a man, he reminded himself.

Beau fussed about Babka's sharp needle. She fussed back in Czech.

After a few moments, Beau spoke again. "If he hadn't barked, I woulda never found Susanna."

The words hit Oscar so hard, they stole the breath from him. He shook his head. "No," he whispered. "No…"

"Where is Toby?" Susanna asked. "I haven't seen him this morning."

"I'm not sure," Beau said quietly. "He's a smart pup. He'll be fine. I'll look for him as soon as Victoria's finished jabbing me with her needle."

"I have only started," Babka muttered. "And already the complaining."

The argument between Beau and his grandmother faded. Instead of listening to them, Oscar imagined the little red dog in the midst of the burning cabin.

He swallowed, trying to loosen the knot in his throat. He pushed off from the doorframe, stumbled across the porch and down the steps. He walked down the muddy path. Tears fell from his eyes, but he didn't bother to wipe them away.

Last night's rain had extinguished most of the fire, but a few stubborn flames burned here and there. They hissed and crackled softly. Aside from the last vestiges of fire, there was no other sound. Just silence. Oscar wanted to call out the dog's name. Toby. He yearned to shout the name across the smoldering ruins, but could find neither the strength nor the will to do so.

167

Chapter Twenty

Beau

Later that day, Beau returned to what remained of the cabin. Smoke wafted from the ashes. Walking around the perimeter, he was struck by the extent of the devastation. He paused to give thanks. The rush of gratitude overwhelmed his thoughts. He knew how close he had come to losing Susanna. He'd come close to losing his own life as well.

Oscar had spent most of the morning walking the property, calling out for Toby. Beau had spent a fair amount of time looking too, but they could not find the dog. Beau assured Oscar that Toby was fine, and that when he got hungry enough, he'd come back. Oscar wasn't convinced and said he'd look more on his own.

Not long before noon, two riders approached. Francine and Holden rode up the path, each child leading a donkey. They stared at the destruction, eyes wide, faces pale.

Beau met them at the path and explained the events of the prior night.

"What are you going to do, Uncle Beau?" Francine asked.

"Are you going to help her rebuild?" Holden added.

"I aim to help as much as she'll let me. We'll see."

Beau didn't elaborate. He had plans and intended to speak to Susanna. All he needed was to make her see the wisdom of his ideas. She needed a man to take charge of things. Surely, she'd find the notion comforting.

They took the donkeys to a paddock near the barn. The donkeys looked to be in fine shape and happy to be home as they trotted around. When they couldn't find their companion, both donkeys brayed and pricked their ears, looking here and there for Rafael.

Holden set his hands on the fence and watched the animals with a smile on his face. "My dad said he sold the other little donkey to a church. A little German church called Saint Joseph's. I think it's one of those painted churches."

"Why would a church need a donkey?" Francine asked.

Holden shrugged.

"You going to go get that one too?" she asked.

"I intend to," Beau replied. "It's mighty important to Susanna."

"If you don't find him there, I can help you put posters up around town," Francine said.

"What do you mean?"

Francine's eyes twinkled. "Isn't that what Rangers do when they're looking for a fugitive? Put up wanted posters?"

Beau shook his head. "I just knew someone would give me grief about looking for donkeys. I can't *believe* it's my own family giving me a bad time."

He looked to Holden for a word of support. The boy's lips twitched with the effort of suppressing a smile.

Francine continued, "I heard that last donkey can give a good kick, Uncle Beau. He's a dangerous type. You're a famous Ranger, but that doesn't mean squat to a shifty outlaw."

Holden snorted. Almost immediately, he looked remorseful, cleared his throat and tried to look serious. Francine's grin widened.

"Shifty outlaw," Beau muttered.

"Yessir. You best be careful with Rafael. He's trouble."

"I'll be sure to keep that in mind, Francine Bailey," Beau said, trying to sound stern.

Beau had to admit he was relieved to share a moment of lighthearted banter. After what had happened last night, it felt good to joke a little. It also gladdened his heart to see the donkeys grazing in the paddock. He could see why Robert Anderson had liked them.

The donkeys' braying had alerted the women. They came to the paddock to see for themselves that the animals had been returned. Susanna's eyes shone with happiness. She'd donned a dress that looked very much as if it belonged to the Novaks. It was somber, dark and had a high collar. Her face was clean. She'd washed and fixed her hair but looked worn out.

Victoria called the donkeys to the fence to offer treats. She brought sugar cubes for Gabriel, and apple for Michael. She fussed over them, petting them tenderly and speaking to them in her native tongue.

"Victoria, these children tell me the third little fella is a dangerous individual." Beau winked at Susanna.

Victoria protested vehemently. She had nothing but praise for all three donkeys. The three were angelic creatures and in no way dangerous.

Francine introduced herself to Susanna. "I'm sorry to hear about your house. I don't want you to pay me for the donkey. I'm happy to bring him back. Seth was grousing about how much he ate."

"That goes the same for me," Holden said.

Susanna stood by the fence, petting the donkeys. She was startled by the offer. It took a moment for her to recover. She shook her head and smiled at the children. "That's very

171

generous. Thank you. I'm a woman of my word. I intend to pay what I owe."

Victoria finished feeding the donkeys and turned to Holden and Francine. "You come inside to eat, yes?"

The children looked pleased by the invitation and nodded.

"I'll take your horses," Beau said. "I'll put them in the barn while we eat."

The children followed Victoria and Elsa back to the Novak house. Beau heard them ask about Oscar. Elsa told them he'd be along soon.

"Can we talk?" Beau asked Susanna.

She agreed. They walked side by side to the barn, neither of them speaking. There were a hundred things Beau considered telling her. The terrible fear he'd felt as he searched for her last night in the smoke. That he'd never prayed so hard in his life. How he'd wanted to hold her all night and every night.

He refused to dwell on foolish notions, however. They entered the barn. Beau loosened the cinch on both horses and tied them to the rail.

"I've decided to stay on," he said, his voice gruffer than he intended. "I can't leave. Not after last night."

"Thank you," she said softly, watching him intently.

He glanced to the back of the barn where he'd built the new bed and done other woodworking. His latest construction stood mostly finished. Bookshelves for all the books that sat packed away in her trunks. He planned to have the shelves ready by now. It turned out to be a good thing he hadn't finished them yet, considering they would have burned along with her books.

"I've got plenty of money, Susanna. My own along with some family money. I can build you a new, better house and then you won't have to spend whatever Robert left for you."

"A new house," she said softly. "I don't want to borrow money from you. I don't want to be indebted."

"I'm not talking about a loan."

"I see." She knit her brow as if she didn't understand any of it.

"I pride myself on doing the right thing," he said. "The honorable thing."

She kept her gaze fixed on him, but still seemed bewildered. He'd expected something different from her. Why didn't she act particularly grateful?

"It's clear you need the help," he said.

She still didn't smile or look happy about his words. Why did she have to make this so difficult?

He went on, trying to clarify. "A *man's* help. Which is why I've decided it would be best if you and I marry."

Her eyes widened and her jaw dropped. "Marry...?"

"That's right." He coaxed his lips into a smile. "I suppose this is where I ask, will you marry me?"

She straightened her shoulders. "You believe proposing is the right thing to do?"

"Now you're getting the idea." He smiled a little more broadly. "That's why I'm here. To serve and protect."

His gaze drifted to her lips which seemed to be pressed together in a grim line, not at all what he imagined. Maybe he'd taken her by surprise. Dang it all, what if she started crying from all the feminine emotions that likely filled her mind?

He worried about this until he realized her tears would offer the perfect chance to take her in his arms once more and he'd certainly enjoyed holding her last night. A rush of warmth came over him as he recalled the way she felt nestled close. They'd fallen asleep together in the early morning hours. The memory of her resting next to him had filled him with deep contentment, especially after the terror of searching for her in the burning cabin.

She'd liked it too. He knew she had, but from the looks of her expression right now, she didn't have fond memories. In fact, she seemed a tad aggravated.

"No thank you," she replied, lifting her chin a notch as she turned to leave the barn.

He stood slack-jawed, watching her stalk out of the barn. It took him a good minute or two before he recovered. Striding after her, he growled a stern command. "Hold up, Susanna. We're not done."

"I think we are." She kept walking.

"You heard Victoria and Elsa. They think we should marry too. Why are you sore? I thought you'd be happy about getting a real, honest-to-goodness proposal."

"I've had a proposal. And for your information Robert's proposal was quite charming."

"Well, this proposal is better."

"What makes you so sure?" She stopped and turned to face him. "Because it's motivated by *duty*, or because it comes from a Ranger?"

"Both, actually."

This got her more riled up and she drew a deep breath to give him a few more pieces of her mind.

Beau spoke before she could get going. "At least this proposal comes from a man who still has all his own teeth."

She didn't seem to appreciate that point either, but at least she didn't blast him with more arguments. Instead, she narrowed her eyes and shook her head. Why, it was as if she was mad at him for offering a simple and perfectly reasonable suggestion they get married.

There was no pleasing some folks.

With a huff of exasperation, she turned on her heel and left him standing there wondering how women could be so difficult to understand.

Chapter Twenty-One

Susanna

The rest of the afternoon, Susanna battled emotions from despair to anger. Perhaps it wasn't fair to be angry with Beau for the way he'd proposed marriage. From the beginning, the man had made it clear he had no use for marriage. He intended to live his life as a Ranger, not tied to a family.

She shouldn't blame him for his deep sense of duty. His sense of duty had driven him to storm into a fire to save her. But later, he'd held her and kissed her so tenderly. It had been her first kiss and swept her into a swirl of giddy emotions. Beau clearly felt none of those pesky feelings.

Beau spent the afternoon working around the ranch. She saw him walk down from the barn to check on the last remnants of the fire. He returned without a word.

The fire had upset everyone, of course. Oscar fretted about the dog. Susanna was certain she heard Toby bark several times around daybreak but couldn't be sure. Oscar searched the ruins. Susanna offered to help but he wanted to be alone.

Victoria fussed about the way he moped. When he came in from searching for several hours, she chided the boy. She spoke in Czech as she kneaded a loaf of bread for their supper. Susanna couldn't understand the exact words but could see the effect they had on the boy. He stood by the window, hiding his tears from the women.

Elsa, who had been quiet for most of the day, erupted with uncharacteristic fury. Susanna was setting the table when Elsa confronted her mother-in-law. The women squared off, facing each other as they debated. Susanna assumed they argued about the dog. Even Oscar was surprised, turning his tear-stained face to the scene that unfolded.

With all the commotion, no one heard the arrival of a horse team and buckboard. A knock at the door stopped the argument. Victoria stood with her flour-covered hands on her waist. Elsa stood by the stove with a ladle in hand. No one moved for a moment. Susanna came to her senses and opened the door to find Fritz Weber.

He looked pale and stricken. Without a word, his gaze went to Elsa. Then to Oscar. He let out a weary but grateful sigh. "I heard about the fire."

Oscar began to respond, but turned away, too overcome to speak. Susanna felt distraught as well. A lump in her throat made it difficult to reply. She drew a shuddering breath and tried to summon an explanation of last night's events.

"We are all fine," Elsa said. "The cabin is lost, of course. As you saw."

"Elsa Novak!" Victoria snapped.

Elsa narrowed her eyes at Victoria and lifted the ladle with a gesture that needed no translation.

"You speak English!" Mr. Weber exclaimed. "I did not know that."

He continued, "I am so glad everyone is okay. I had imagined the worst of things."

Elsa lowered the ladle. "The little dog helped Susanna and Beau last night. He barked and showed Beau the way. There was so much smoke."

Mr. Weber nodded. He swallowed hard and turned to look at Oscar. The boy's shoulders shook.

"Toby is a smart dog. He saved Susanna and Beau." Elsa set the ladle aside. "We are lucky to have him."

Victoria grumbled and turned back to the bread on the counter. She resumed kneading the dough, working with a pronounced vigor.

Elsa ignored her. When she spoke again, her breath caught in her throat. Her gaze went from Oscar, to Mr. Weber and back to Oscar. "But...it seems..."

"We cannot find the dog, Mr. Weber," Susanna said. "Oscar has searched all day to no avail."

"Ach, yes. Perhaps I can help find little Toby." Mr. Weber's face brightened.

"Go, Oscar. You and Mr. Weber can work together," Elsa said.

"Yes, Mama," Oscar said, quietly.

"I hope you find Toby," she said. "A boy should have a dog. Especially a good dog."

Victoria was silent, but anger flashed behind her eyes. Elsa gave her a pointed look as if daring her to argue. Oscar looked surprised by the exchange. Perhaps a tiny bit less heartbroken.

Mr. Weber turned to leave but stopped on the porch. He came back to the door. "I almost forgot. There is a letter for Mrs. Anderson."

He gave her an envelope and left with Oscar. Elsa went to the door and watched from there, quiet and thoughtful. Victoria resumed kneading the dough. Susanna opened the letter.

The letter came from Henry and the sight of his handwriting pleased her tremendously. She'd come to Texas, partly in hopes of a new life for Henry, but had to admit she'd hardly thought of all her grand plans. Since arriving in Sweet Willow, her life had been a whirlwind, different tasks pulling her in various directions.

She was grateful for the letter even though it brought a wave of loneliness as she thought of Henry so far away. His note gave her a welcome respite from the series of calamities. The short letter was dated just a few days after she'd left Albany. To her surprise, her father had dismissed Henry. She could only imagine how angry Hubert Astor had been to fire his butler. It was probably for the best, however.

His letter took a more serious note with a passage about her father. Susanna wasn't surprised that her father didn't miss her and seemed pleased that she'd left.

Edgar Wiggins, on the other hand, is quite outraged that you jilted him. Somehow, he learned that you traveled to Sweet Willow and makes all sorts of threats about sending thugs to Texas to haul you back. He ignores the fact that you have a husband...

Susanna's heart plunged to her feet. Edgar Wiggins. How horrible to read his name in Henry's letter. Aunt Molly must have told her friends about Sweet Willow. Molly wouldn't have been able to resist bragging of the trick she'd played on her detestable brother-in-law. She'd probably gloated at one of her parties. Word had spread. How else could Edgar Wiggins know the name of a small town in Texas?

Molly had boasted. Of course, she had.

"What's the matter?" Elsa asked.

Susanna's mouth went dry. Her thoughts spun inside her mind. How could she explain the details of her life in Albany? To the Novak ladies, family was everything. Neither would understand a father who schemed to exchange his only child for a debt. Or a father who had assumed she would not live long and helped himself to her inheritance. Nor would they grasp how Aunt Molly must have betrayed Susanna's secret.

She stared at them, unsure how to explain all the troubles the letter contained.

Victoria poured a cup of water and tried to offer it to Susanna.

Susanna shook her head. "This is t-terrible. Awful. I don't know what to d-do."

The women shared a look of concern. Susanna began with Henry's message. Then she tried to explain what her father had done. The women frowned, unable to understand any part of her story.

The more she spoke, the more she stumbled over her words.

Victoria urged her to take a drink of the water. Elsa tried to coax her to the chair. Susanna grew more distraught.

"I didn't think this d-day could get any worse," Susanna cried. "I feel utterly l-lost. I should never have come to Sweet W-Willow."

The women understood this part. Both looked stricken.

Elsa snatched the water from Victoria. Susanna shook her head, too overwrought to explain that a drink would hardly help. Elsa didn't offer the water, however. Instead, she threw the water at Susanna's face.

Susanna blinked. The water dripped down her face. The Novak ladies spoke quietly. Victoria expressed dismay, while Elsa clearly felt no remorse for what she'd done. Victoria went to the sink and returned with a towel. Susanna dried her face.

"Better?" Victoria asked.

Susanna was indignant. How could a reasonable, kind-hearted woman like Elsa treat her so rudely? Who would do such a thing? Elsa Novak didn't even look remorseful. Susanna wanted to give her a piece of her mind. Despite her outrage, she realized that the panic had subsided. The relief felt like an enormous weight had been lifted from her chest. Instead of terror, she felt strangely calm.

She let out a murmur of surprise. "I suppose I am a little better."

Elsa smiled.

Chapter Twenty-Two

Oscar

Oscar stared at the ruins of Mr. Anderson's house. He'd spent most of the day wandering around what was left of the cabin. Earlier, he couldn't bear to stop searching. Now he felt tired and hopeless.

Mr. Weber strolled around the pile of smoking ashes. He called the dog, whistled, and peered into the bushes and shrubs. When he noticed Oscar watching him, he smiled good-naturedly. The man's optimism irritated Oscar.

"I know you left the dog here," Oscar said.

Mr. Weber shrugged.

"Why did you do that?"

"I think a boy should have a dog if he wants one."

Oscar could hardly argue with that. He wasn't the one objecting to a dog, after all. It was Babka who complained about them. Their smell. The fur. The barking. His grandmother had nothing good to say about dogs.

Mr. Weber continued his search for the dog.

Beau called out a greeting from the barn. He walked down the path, his expression dark. He looked as irritated as Oscar felt. Everyone was in a bad mood, it seemed. Even Mama and Babka quarreled. While the two women often debated matters, all matters, it seemed to him, they rarely got angry with each other. Babka and Mama were as close as mother and daughter and that was the way Oscar liked things. Peaceful.

Today, the two women argued more loudly than usual. He didn't like to hear them or see either of them so upset. It seemed as though everything was bad today.

Still, his mother had said they were lucky to have Toby and that a boy should have a dog. Just as Mr. Weber had said. Maybe that's why his mother had changed her mind. Anyway, it didn't matter. Not anymore.

Beau shook hands with Mr. Weber. The two men spoke of the fire and the terrible loss. They talked more of how what mattered was that everyone was safe. Oscar curled his hands into fists. He wanted to shout that not everyone had come out of the fire unscathed. He kicked a rock. It arced in the air and landed in a bush.

A sound came from the shrub. A yelp of pain.

Mr. Weber spun around. "What was that?"

"I don't know," Oscar replied. He remained still, rooted to the spot.

The branches moved. The leaves rustled. Toby emerged. He looked around, bewildered.

Oscar stared, hardly daring to breathe or trust his eyes.

When the dog spied Oscar, he barked and scampered over. His coat, usually a deep copper, was covered in dark ash. A few feet from Oscar, the dog stopped to shake himself, causing a cloud of soot to waft into the air.

Beau and Mr. Weber were almost as happy as Oscar. They made a fuss over the dog and, together, they managed to give the pup a bath. Not an easy task. Toby wriggled and protested the bath. Twice, he escaped the bucket of suds. Mr. Weber and Oscar had to chase after him. By the time they were done, everyone was wet and smiling ear to ear. Best of all, Toby was back to his pretty copper color.

Mama came out to see the dog, along with Susanna.

Even Babka came to see what the fuss was about. She looked stern and forbidding, not at all happy about the little dog. Ignoring it, she squared her shoulders and, to Oscar's utter shock, spoke to Mr. Weber. In English.

"You must eat supper," she said, her tone stiff. "With us."

It took Mr. Weber a moment to reply. He reddened as he yanked his hat from his head. His mouth opened and closed a time or two. Beau looked almost as surprised as Mr. Weber but managed to recover enough to pat the man on the shoulder.

Mr. Weber came to his senses. "It would be an honor."

Babka gave a brittle nod.

"I like Czech food very much," he added.

His grandmother had no response to this comment. Oscar could just imagine what went through Babka's mind. Of course, he liked the food. Didn't everyone? Mr. Weber might have said something like the sky was blue. Or the grass was green.

Oscar couldn't help feeling a little sorry for Mr. Weber. If only there were some way to warn the man. Babka might have invited him to supper, but that didn't mean she approved of him.

No, it meant that over the next hour or two, she would watch his every move. And she would remember. Later that evening, his grandmother would list the man's bad manners. It would be a topic of discussion for months, possibly longer.

Mama smiled, her eyes shining with happiness. She might think she'd won a long-standing argument with Babka. She hadn't. Babka was simply gathering fuel for her fire, a little blaze she'd keep going for as long as it suited her.

Oscar felt a little sorry for his mother, too. Whenever his mother saw Mr. Weber, she always got a soft look in her eyes, making her look much younger than her years. The few times he'd seen his mother look like that, he'd been unhappy, but today, with Toby still alive, he didn't much care how his mother looked at Mr. Weber.

The little dog was safe. That was enough. God heard his prayers.

Chapter Twenty-Three

Beau

To Beau's surprise, dinner with Mr. Weber went well. The Novaks treated him with the utmost hospitality. Fritz Weber knew just how to play his cards. Each time Victoria brought a dish to the table, he'd gone on about how beautiful the dish looked, and how it smelled so heavenly, and how everything about the meal up to that point had been the best he'd ever eaten. By the time Elsa served dessert, a type of honey cake, Victoria was almost amiable.

Just before Fritz took his first taste of the cake, he mentioned something which changed everything. His great-grandmother had come from a town in the old country that neighbored the Novak's hometown.

The news caused quite a stir amongst the Novak family. Elsa smiled. Oscar looked incredulous. Victoria took out a small bottle of spirits she kept tucked away. She couldn't convince Elsa to drink any, or anyone else other than Fritz. She poured the spirits into special glasses, delicate crystal glasses. They were from the famous Bohemian glass shops of her homeland. Victoria held them up to the candlelight to show off the fine work of the Bohemian craftsmen.

Later that night, after Fritz had left and Beau left the Novak's cabin, he resolved to check the burned cabin. A wind stirred. Beau wanted to be certain there were no hot spots that might spark a new blaze. There was little left to burn. Just the same, he wanted to see with his own eyes.

A walk might help the restlessness stirring inside him. It was none of the usual disquiet he felt when he stayed in one place too long. To his great surprise, he had no desire to leave.

He walked around the ruins, a lantern in one hand and a spade in the other. He jabbed the prongs of the spade into the ash. Each time, he searched for sparks or embers.

Victoria came from her cabin, carrying a lantern. "Everything is all right?"

"It's fine. I couldn't sleep. Thought I'd make sure the fire was out."

Beau grimaced as he recalled the events of the day. Susanna had barely spoken to him that evening. He was in for a long night of tossing and turning while she probably slept like a baby tucked in a spare bed at the Novak's cabin.

That evening, when he'd given the two donkeys a little grain, she'd come to the fence to watch. She'd cooed and made a fuss over the animals, scratching behind their ears. She had scarcely a word for him, though, despite the fact that he'd helped her find the donkeys and was feeding them too. In his irritation, he'd turned his back on one of them and got bit. Before he could escape the pen, another one landed a well-placed kick on his shin. Had Susanna noticed or cared? No. She had either not noticed or not cared. Maybe both.

He rubbed his forearm, wincing at the pain. That Gabriel was no angel. Michael wasn't any better. Darned donkeys. They still needed to find Rafael and he was supposed to be the finicky one.

Victoria found a stick and began prodding the ashes. "I hear you in the barn working."

188

"That's right. I'm working on some bookshelves for Susanna."

Victoria's lantern cast a soft glow across her features. Her lips curved with a smile. Susanna had probably told her about the proposal. Or maybe Victoria guessed. There was no telling.

"You change your mind about Fritz?" Beau asked, his tone edging on resentful.

"He's a good man."

"Now that you know he's one of your countrymen?"

Victoria's smile broadened.

The wind picked up, swirling little eddies of ash. Beau peered into the ash, searching for a glow from a spark or ember. Nothing, thankfully.

Beau walked the perimeter twice more to make certain the fire had died. He set the spade aside. Victoria stood quietly, her lantern in hand, gazing into the darkness. She still wore a slight smile as she pondered.

"I suppose Fritz is sweet on Elsa," Beau said.

Victoria nodded. "I know. And she is sweet on Fritz."

Beau braced himself for a tirade, but none came.

"Elsa looked happy," Victoria said quietly.

"She's been a widow a long time."

"She and my son were married only four months before he died. I thought about that tonight after he left. Four months is nothing. At least I had my husband, Josef, for twenty years."

Victoria's voice held a deep note of sorrow. Beau knew she rarely showed a shred of vulnerability. Her usual manner was steely, unwavering, determined. It was as though she alone carried the mantle of family responsibility. It was up to her to keep the Novaks together and she intended to do so through sheer force of will.

"Elsa is still young," Beau said. "What, maybe thirty-five?"

"Thirty-seven."

"She's got a lot of living still to do. Might get a little lonesome when Oscar goes off to school."

Victoria winced. The notion of Oscar leaving the fold visibly pained her. Beau wanted to point out that she was the one harping on the boy becoming a doctor. It seemed no one had asked Oscar what he wanted.

"Fritz is a good man. He's never been married. I don't believe he's even courted a girl. He's always working, running the mercantile. He's not the sort of man who chases skirts."

Victoria frowned. "Chases skirts?"

"Fritz isn't a lady's man. He doesn't toy with women's hearts. He's sweet on Elsa and you can bet this is the first time he's tried to win a lady's affections." Beau chuckled. "Poor Fritz. He finally tries to court a girl and her mother-in-law is Victoria Novak."

Victoria lifted her chin a notch. Beau half-expected her to turn the tables on him and start talking about offering for Susanna. She'd made no secret about her opinion. He should quit his work for the Rangers. Stay in Sweet Willow and marry Susanna. She'd said those very words every single day, several times a day. Just in case he'd missed some part of her meaning the first fifty times.

"How is your arm?" she asked.

"It's fine. You did a good job stitching me up."

"Your other arm. Where Gabriel bite you."

"Susanna told you about that, did she?"

In the soft light of the lantern, Victoria's eyes sparkled with amusement. "He kicked you too, yes?"

"Like you don't already know about that. Yes, he did kick me. I wasn't paying good attention. I was a little distracted."

She nodded, a smile curving her lips. He could tell she was reading all sorts of nonsense into his mention of distracted. He rubbed the spot where he'd been bitten, scowling as he imagined the women talking about the incident and laughing at his expense.

He thinned his lips. "Did Mrs. Anderson tell you I asked her to marry me? Did she get to that part, or did she just tell the story about the dang donkeys?"

"She told us."

"Us?"

"While you checked the fire." She gestured toward the pile of ash. "She told me, Elsa, Fritz, Oscar...Toby."

"Toby the dog knows about my proposal?" He shook his head. "Now you're just being mean, Victoria."

She lifted her hand to her mouth to hide her laughter, not bothering to deny his words.

"I'm trying to do the right thing," Beau argued. "I want to stay, to marry Susanna, to take care of her."

"You can tell her this, but you must also tell her how you feel." She set her hand on her heart. "Tell her you care for her."

Beau rubbed the back of his neck. How had he ended up getting advice from Victoria Novak about how to propose?

"I told her I want to stay to protect her. I'm not sure what's left to say."

"To protect her?"

"That's right. Isn't it clear that's what I want?"

Victoria gazed at him for a long moment before sighing deeply. He'd disappointed her. Well, wasn't that just dandy. His proposal was bad enough to warrant disapproval from Victoria Novak.

191

"Maybe you need protection," she said, a sly smile tugging at the corner of her mouth.

He scoffed. "Doubtful."

She eyed him thoughtfully.

"I'm the one who protects, Victoria. I've always been that way, just like my father and his father. It's how I was raised. It's part of my family's credo. Protect others, especially women and children."

Shrugging, she turned to leave. "Maybe so. But today you got a very bad cut, stitches, kicked *and* bitten."

Before he could reply, she lifted her hand to stop him.

"You marry to protect each other. Because together you are stronger. Better."

He couldn't argue that point.

"Two are better than one. If one falls, the other can lift."

She tapped her chin as if trying to recall some detail. Her words stirred some hazy memory. He tried to make sense of the recollection. Wisps of his childhood returned. Sunday school. Bible study. It dawned on him that Victoria quoted the Bible. She wasn't trying to remember a passage but trying to translate verse.

"And so," she continued her brow furrowed with the strain of translating. "If two peoples lie down near each other, they will be warm. You know? And one person alone is not warm."

"Ecclesiastes."

"*Ano.*" She nodded. "Yes."

With that she bid him good night and began the walk back to her cabin. Beau remained where he stood, watching as the light from her lantern faded into the darkness.

One person alone is not warm...

For what had to be the hundredth time, he thought about the way Susanna felt, tucked in his embrace last night after he'd found her in the fire. She felt right, more than right. She felt perfect, as if she belonged there and he missed her scent, and soft, feminine shape and everything about her.

He knew Victoria was right.

Victoria's kind-hearted attempt to translate the quote from the Bible moved his heart. If only he could persuade Susanna they'd be better together. Even more important, could he convince her that the two of them were meant to be man and wife?

Chapter Twenty-Four

Susanna

Two days after the fire, Seth and Noah came to see Beau. They'd heard about the fire and wanted to see if their cousin needed anything. Beau introduced her to the men when they drove up to the Novak cabin.

Noah had been by the post office before coming and had a letter for Susanna. It was from Molly. Susanna smiled and thanked him as she tucked it in her pocket.

To her surprise, Seth had something for her too. A gift from his wife, Laura. A new dress.

"Laura heard the fire took everything. She fretted about your wardrobe, of course. She's one for pretty things. She wanted to come herself to say hello," Seth explained. "The baby was fussy with a new tooth."

Susanna held the dress up for Victoria and Elsa to admire. The two women marveled at the fine workmanship. The dress was a lovely periwinkle with ruched sleeves and a narrow bodice. It looked as though it would fit but if not, she'd get Elsa's help to make alterations.

"I don't know what to say." Susanna felt a rush of gratitude. She'd lost everything in the fire. As much as she appreciated Elsa's dress, it was dark and somber, suited for mourning just like everything the Novak women wore.

"Laura enjoys making pretty dresses," Seth said, his voice edged with pride. "She used to make a pretty penny for her work back in Boston. Now she likes to give dresses to her friends and family."

Susanna's face heated. She wasn't sure if she fit in the friend category or the family category. Beau regarded her without saying a word. Ever since he'd proposed, he'd kept his distance. He was polite but nothing more.

"Sorry to hear about the cabin, Mrs. Anderson," Noah said.

Susanna nodded. "Thank you. I'm still having a hard time believing it's gone."

The group grew quiet. Everyone seemed to agree. The men gazed at the burned remains of the cabin. They shook their head with dismay.

Susanna smiled at Oscar who stood by Beau. "Oscar has been working hard on new plans. He's quite talented."

The men turned their attention to the boy. Oscar reddened. He waved a dismissive hand.

"He's sketched plans for a new cabin," Susanna said.

"You don't say," Noah marveled. "I've heard you've got a good head for numbers. You know more math than the two schoolteachers. And that's saying something. Bess and Gertie Payne are plum smart ladies."

"Oscar will be a doctor," Victoria said.

"If he wants to be a doctor," Elsa added.

The two ladies began a heated debate as they drifted back inside.

"I just built a house," Noah said. "I needed the room for my growing family. I can give you the list of men who worked for me."

Susanna nodded. "Thank you."

She excused herself, eager to read Molly's letter. The men went to the remains of the cabin to see the extent of the devastation. Oscar went with them, Toby on his heels.

Inside the cabin, she laid the new dress on the bed. She returned to the sitting room to read Molly's letter. The letter was brief. Most of it revolved around Molly's complaints. She mentioned that Henry had received a letter, but from someone other than Susanna. At the very end of the letter, she included a quick note that Edgar Wiggins had married.

The oaf wed some poor unsuspecting girl from Philadelphia...

Susanna let out a breath of relief. Thank goodness. She wasn't sure if the man had truly contemplated making the trip to Texas to find her, but the mere idea had terrified her. She'd suffered bad dreams about Edgar Wiggins coming for her.

She could set aside her worries now. With Mr. Wiggins married, the threat was gone. He'd probably found a girl who still had a little money to her name. Susanna was grateful. She felt liberated. It was as if she was free from a long-standing menace.

Elsa and Victoria paused their discussion for a moment, both eyeing her with curiosity.

Susanna recalled the incident of a few days ago when Elsa had tossed a cup of water in her face.

"Are you wondering if it's bad news?" Susanna asked, a smile tugging at her lips.

Elsa folded her arms across her chest. "Yes. Is it? I hope not."

Susanna shook her head. "It is not. Thankfully. But I do owe my aunt a letter."

Victoria brought her ink and paper. "You write. Your aunt will want to know that you are well."

The two women left the cabin to work in the garden. Susanna could hear them talking as they continued their debate outside. She opened the ink well, dipped her pen in the ebony fluid and began her letter. She resolved to tell Molly about the land and the people too, of course. She added a few details about Beau, trying not to say too much about the man. Molly would only jump to conclusions.

About the fire, Susanna said nothing. It wouldn't be prudent. Molly would worry unnecessarily. Perhaps when the new construction was completed, she'd tell her the story. Not now.

A sound distracted her from the letter. Toby barked. He sounded as though he was on the porch. His bark sounded more fierce than usual. It surprised Susanna both by the intensity and that the dog was on the porch instead of traipsing around after Oscar. Ever since the fire, Toby hadn't been more than a few paces from the boy. Oscar had even managed to convince Victoria to let him take the dog into the loft to sleep.

Susanna rose from her chair and went to the door, intending to quiet the dog. When she opened the door, she found a man standing at the threshold. She gasped. He was a stranger. He kicked at Toby who darted away, avoiding the blow.

The man turned to her, glowering, his face red with rage. "You burned down my cabin."

Susanna staggered back. "Your cabin?"

"That's right. It belongs to me." The man followed, slamming the door behind him. Toby scratched the door, barking frantically.

"Who are you?" Susanna demanded as she retreated several more steps.

"I'm Jack Anderson. This is my family's property. I've come to claim the land before you burn anything else down."

"I didn't burn anything. It wasn't my fault."

She backed away from the man. He advanced, his eyes bulging with anger. A smell emanated from him, a stale odor that seemed vaguely familiar. Slowly it dawned on her. It was the same stench that clung to Edgar Wiggins, the smell of drink. Not the fruity scent of a glass of wine but the rancid smell a man who had consumed too much for too long.

He took a few steps closer, looming over her. "Of course, it's your fault. It was standing when you got here, wasn't it?"

Susanna pursed her lips. A deep well of anger filled her chest. His words. His demeanor. His bullying. It was all too much.

"Answer me," he roared. "Was it, or was it not standing?"

"It was standing." She surprised herself with her calm response.

"And now it's burned to the ground." He lurched unsteadily, spittle gathering on his lips.

"Yes, that's true." She retreated another step, stopping when she reached the table.

"So, that means you're to blame. You. A stranger. You weren't even married proper-like to Robert Anderson."

His gaze drifted from her face, down the length of her body. "Maybe you and me should get married. I'd make certain to marry you properly. Nothing convenient about taking a wife like you."

He gave a lewd chuckle. Rubbing his jaw, he arched his brow suggestively.

A shudder of revulsion ran along her spine. Jack Anderson was disgusting. Indeed. It was no wonder that Robert disliked the man. She'd known Jack all of two minutes and regretted ever laying eyes on him. She waved her hand in front of her nose trying to waft away the man's disagreeable odor.

He snarled, baring his tobacco-stained teeth.

"I'm afraid I'll have to decline the offer," Susanna replied. "Despite the charming wording."

"If you ain't married, you're fair game." He stepped closer and leered at her.

"Fair game?"

"That's right."

"Be still my beating heart."

Jack blinked. He cocked his head to one side. "What?"

"Fair game, you say? What a romantic notion. How can a girl resist?"

His lips curved into a smile as he pondered her comment. "You think I'm romantic?"

The man seemed to think she was sincerely complimenting him.

"I can't be the only one to suggest such a thing."

She glanced out the window, searching for someone who might offer help. The yard was empty. She was alone with man who was twice her size.

She had stopped his advance, but for how long? He looked as if he intended to throw her over his shoulder and carry her off to exchange vows. She eyed his filthy hands. Her gaze drifted to the stains on his shirt and the way his smile made him look particularly cruel.

Audentes fortuna iuvat...

Henry's words returned to her mind. Fortune favors the bold...

She didn't want to compliment Jack Anderson. She wanted to make clear he'd trespassed, and taken something that didn't belong to him. He'd deliberately defied his uncle's wishes. She wanted to make clear she wouldn't let him or any other man bully her.

"You stole my donkeys," she said softly.

"Your donkeys?"

"You sold them at the auction."

His smile vanished. "You can't talk to me like that, girl," he snarled.

Her thoughts moved to Molly. Her bravery. Her audacious display on her front step when she ran off the trio of thugs.

Elsa's kind face came to mind. Susanna trailed her fingers along the edge of the table. Her fingertips brushed against what she sought.

"Get off my ranch, Jack."

"Your ranch?" he bellowed.

She nodded, gently clasping the object on the table. "And never, ever come back."

"Why you little-" He lunged for her. She swung the inkpot, hurling the contents into the face of Jack Anderson. The black ink splashed across his startled expression. He screamed and fell to the floor. The crash rattled the windows. He writhed and roared.

From outside came a response from both man and beast. The air filled with shouts. Yelling. Barking.

She stood still, motionless, her fingers clasped around the dripping inkwell.

The door burst open. Beau stood in the doorway, his eyes flashing with fury. He strode into the cabin, the two other Baileys a few steps behind. Without a word, he yanked Jack Anderson off the floor and hauled him outside.

A moment later, Victoria and Elsa burst through the door. Both women paled. Oscar hurried to the cabin. Toby bounded around barking one minute, whining and crying the next.

201

Susanna had to admit she felt much like the little dog, not sure if she was elated or overwrought.

Over the next few hours, her shock dissipated, and a sense of relief came over her. Seth and Noah Bailey took Jack Anderson into town, to deliver him to the sheriff of Sweet Willow. Beau prowled around like a lion with a thorn in his paw, angered and looking to vent his frustration.

Later that evening, while the Novaks prepared for bed, Susanna found him outside their cabin leaning against the porch railing. It was a dark, moonless night. A soft breeze stirred. While most of the porch lay in shadows, light from the cabin cast a warm glow across the porch corner. He took off his cowboy hat and came part way across the porch.

Beau was always gallant, always polite. He never failed to get to his feet when she or one of the Novak ladies spoke. He did so out of respect to women. He took off his hat for the same reason. He showed his usual good manners. But he still reminded her of the proverbial wounded lion. Brooding with a considerable bit of unspent anger that simmered just below the surface.

His restlessness hadn't subsided even though Jack Anderson had been gone for half the day. His family credo ran deep. He was driven to serve and protect, but his need to take care of *her* ran deeper. She knew that now.

"Are you going to sleep out here?" she asked, gently teasing.

"Not sure," he replied, his voice gruff.

"You mean you're considering it?"

"More like I'm not sure if I can sleep at all."

"I feel quite the opposite. As though I'll fall asleep the moment my head hits the pillow."

His expression softened. "Go on to sleep. I'll be nearby if you need me."

He left the porch, vanishing into the shadows.

"I need you..." she said, too softly for him to hear.

Chapter Twenty-Five

Beau

Early the next morning, Noah and Holden came to the ranch, leading the last donkey. Beau met them at the paddock gate where the other two donkeys brayed and fussed to see their companion. When Beau opened the gate, Rafael trotted into the paddock to join Michael and Gabriel.

Noah and Holden didn't stay long. Before they left, Beau gave his cousin a letter he'd written the night before.

"I'd be grateful if you could mail it today," Beau said. "I'm giving my notice to my commanding officer. I'm quitting the Rangers. Retiring after fifteen years' service."

Noah grinned. "Glad to hear."

"I've been meaning to write for some time. I have more money than I need after saving my salary and what my grandfather left me. I'm ready to make it official."

Noah arched a brow, glancing around the property. "Are you going to make it official with Mrs. Anderson?"

"I intend to. She's pretty stubborn."

Noah laughed as he tucked the letter in his pocket. "Let us know what we can do. You're family. If you're settling down, it would be a good reason to celebrate."

Beau nodded and bid them good-bye. He walked up the path to the Novak's cabin, pleased that all three donkeys were finally back on the property. He hadn't cared too much for the donkeys in the beginning, but they were important to Susanna, which meant they were important to him.

He looked forward to telling her that the last one had come home.

Even though he hadn't slept a wink, he didn't feel at all tired. He was eager to speak to Susanna, to propose properly this time, to make up for the sorry marriage offer he'd given her a few days ago.

When he knocked on the Novak's door, Susanna opened it, her eyes lit with surprise. She was dressed, not in the dark, somber dress Elsa had given her after the fire but the brightly colored dress Laura had brought. Her hair hung loose around her shoulders and tumbled down her back. He'd never seen it unbound and was momentarily struck by the sight.

Susanna was beautiful.

He thought that all the time, but even more so that morning. He rubbed his palm across his scars, conscious of his rough appearance. All night, he'd imagined this moment. In his mind, it had gone perfectly. She'd accepted his proposal. Eagerly. Now he felt tongue-tied. An unpleasant prickle crawled across his skin.

Fortunately, one of the donkeys brayed, reminding him of Rafael's arrival. Beau had a good excuse to invite Susanna on a short walk before breakfast. Silently, he noted a sense of gratitude. The donkeys, for the first time, had contributed something helpful.

"I've got something to show you," he said.

A smile curved her lips. "All right."

She waited, looking at him expectantly.

"It's in the pasture." He gestured to her feet. "You need to put some boots on, unless you want me to carry you."

"That would be a long way," she teased. Turning to look back over her shoulder, she said a few words to Victoria. After she closed the door, she sat on a chair on the porch and pulled on Elsa's boots, a battered pair of dark work boots that had seen better days.

"I wouldn't mind," he said. "Carrying you, that is." He winced. This wasn't going all that well.

The part about not minding was true, however. He'd held her in his arms before and would have relished the chance to do it again, preferably not as he walked through the smoke and flames of a burning cabin. It would suit him better to carry Susanna over a threshold after saying their vows.

They began down the trail to the corral. He took her hand and tucked it in the crook of his arm. She looked up at him, a soft rosy blush coloring her pretty face.

"You reckon Victoria and Elsa are watching?" he asked.

"I'm almost certain." Her color deepened. "Maybe Oscar and Toby too."

He smiled and squeezed her hand. The three little donkeys waited, watching them as they approached, their heads over the top rail of the gate. They flicked their ears and gave soft whickers. Two oaks stood on either side of the gate, arching their branches across the span.

"Oh my goodness," Susanna exclaimed. "You got Rafael back."

"Noah brought him this morning."

When they got to the gate, Susanna pet the new donkey. Rafael was the smallest but also the fuzziest. He had a splotch of white on his forehead that gave him a mischievous look. His forelock was a short frazzle of hair that blew in the breeze.

"He's darling," Susanna said.

Beau wasn't so sure. The other two were far from darling and he wanted to reserve judgement on the littlest. Sometimes the smallest of anything was the quickest and meanest.

"Thank you, Beau," Susanna said, looking up at him. "For everything."

"I'm happy to do it."

Sparks of amusement danced in her eyes. "I know. I know. You like to serve and protect."

"That's not it."

She gave him a curious look. "Because you like donkeys?"

He shook his head. "Not that either."

"It's Victoria's cooking, isn't it?"

He cupped her shoulders and gazed into the depths of her gray eyes. "I do what I do because I love you. That's why."

She blinked, her smile fading.

"And I want to marry you so I can serve and protect, but also because I want to be with you from first thing in the morning until I fall asleep at night. I want to be with you forever, to grow old with you, and, God willing, have children and grandchildren."

She swallowed and nodded. He stroked her jaw with his thumb. "Will you marry me, Susanna?"

"I will, Beau. Nothing would make me happier."

Chapter Twenty-Six

Susanna

Henry and Molly's arrival in Sweet Willow came as such a surprise that Susanna was unable to summon a single word for a quarter hour. It happened the evening after Beau asked her to marry. A buggy arrived from Sweet Willow, with Henry and Molly sitting in the back.

Beau and Susanna walked to the path to greet the visitors.

Molly shouted greetings from a hundred yards away, giving the donkeys quite a fright. They'd bolted, galloping away into the pasture. Toby barked and fussed. The Novaks came running from the garden.

"What a charming home," Molly proclaimed. "Isn't it charming, Henry?"

Henry looked a little dazed from the trip. "Charming." He pointed to the remains of Robert's cabin. "What happened there?"

"It's a story," said Susanna, "a long one. Let me tell you sometime when you've rested."

Henry took hold of Susanna's hands. "My heart broke for you when I read that your husband Mr. Anderson had passed before you'd even met him. I'm so sorry for you, my dear."

He folded Susanna into his embrace. He held her for a long while, finally stepping back to look at her with tears in his eyes. "My girl. I've missed you so."

"And I've missed you, both of you, so much."

Susanna introduced Molly and Henry to Beau and the Novak family. The Novak women promptly set to preparing food for the visitors, while Susanna and Beau showed Henry and Molly the gardens and orchards, and the donkeys.

As they admired the donkeys, Susanna said, "Beau has asked me to marry him."

Henry eyed Beau.

Molly did too, but almost at once smiled approvingly. "I'm so glad. She'll need a man's help and you look quite capable."

"Beau was a Texas Ranger," Susanna said.

"A Ranger," Henry marveled. "A lawman?"

"Yes sir. I just gave my notice. I aim to be a family man, at home with Susanna."

After that, Henry was all smiles. He approved of Beau's desire to be a family man. In addition, Henry had read about Rangers and held them in high regard. Beau's comments earned extra points in Henry's book. Susanna could see that clear as day.

The next morning, Beau went to town to talk to the preacher. He said he'd do whatever it took to have the wedding on the next Saturday. A few hours later, he was back, his smile so broad and joyful that everyone knew without asking that everything had been arranged.

Over the next week, Susanna showed Henry and Molly around the ranch, taking their time to truly appreciate the beauty of Texas in October. Henry commented on the fine temperatures and long days, and how he could get used to all the sunshine. Beau said that sounded fine, but he should reserve judgement on Texas weather until the following July and August, when the sun and heat tended to wear out their welcome.

Beau, Oscar and Henry talked about the plans for the new cabin, discussing all the finer details such as where the sun rose and set, and the advantages and disadvantages of facing the front door south or north. They also considered that Oscar's original design might need to be expanded, now that there was talk of marriage and, hopefully, children.

The Novaks prepared meals and enjoyed hearing Henry and Molly's stories of New York. Victoria was particularly impressed by Henry's forty years of service to the Astor family, continuing to serve the family even after the death of Susanna's mother, to shepherd and protect Susanna from her angry father. She said that Henry's devotion to his work reminded her of her own father, and that she was thankful to prepare food and share meals with such a good man. Oscar and Elsa seemed speechless to hear Victoria praise Henry's character, and more than once Susanna heard them ask if Henry might have some Czech in his blood.

The day of the wedding, Susanna awoke at dawn. Victoria had already heated water for her bath. Elsa made a hasty breakfast and woke Oscar, telling him to take his breakfast outside and that he wasn't allowed in the house until Susanna had left the house.

He'd grumbled, but he was no match for Victoria. It was tradition, she told him, "No men in the house while the bride dresses for her wedding."

Oscar, his hair mussed, still dressed in his long night shirt, wandered to the front porch toting a blanket, yawning, with Toby on his heels. The boy settled on the swing and went right back to sleep. The dog curled up beside the swing and went back to sleep as well.

Elsa laid out the wedding dress that Susanna was to wear. Laura Bailey had made the dress for Susanna, a delicate, ivory frock with a matching veil. Even the Novak ladies, who were usually tight-lipped when it came to praise, marveled at the lovely dress.

Not only had Laura made the dress quickly, she'd managed to make it while having Molly in her home. Molly was not the type of woman to spend time by herself. She required a lot of maintenance, and Susanna was thankful for Laura and Seth's hospitality.

Molly, still fascinated with birds, had lately concluded she preferred to see them in the wild rather than in cages. She'd read about the birds of Galveston Island and planned to travel to the coast and stay in a grand hotel with a group of other ladies to observe the migrating birds.

"She's become an avid bird watcher," Henry told Susanna one morning over breakfast. He'd sighed wearily. "Try not to get her started on the subject."

Henry, who needed very little in the way of maintenance, had bunked with Beau.

The prior evening, Molly had offered to come help Susanna with her dress and hair. Susanna didn't respond right away. She pictured the scene and it seemed like a bad idea. Molly wasn't the type of woman who helped other women dress. In her home in Albany, she had her own regiment of upstairs maids.

Elsa, thank goodness, had intervened, telling Molly she should rest before the wedding, and that she and Victoria would love nothing more than to help Susanna. Thankfully, Molly conceded.

Now that the time to prepare had come, Susanna was grateful to have help from the Novak ladies. They were calm, efficient and thoughtful.

Victoria brought Susanna a cup of tea and a biscuit. "Eat something, Susanna."

"Yes, ma'am," Susanna said.

Victoria brushed a lock of hair from Susanna's eyes and smiled. "Your hair is a very pretty color. Like a shiny penny. You will look so beautiful today."

"A beautiful bride," Elsa added with a wistful note in her voice.

As the ladies helped her dress, they joked about Beau's suit. Victoria ironed the shirt the night before. Beau hadn't argued about it and seemed grateful, much to Victoria's astonishment.

They discussed the wedding preparations, particularly about the reception to be held in the church hall. Susanna had let the woman handle the festivities following the vows, a task they seemed very pleased to take out off her hands.

"Fritz Weber invited a band," Elsa said.

Susanna expected Victoria to grumble about Fritz, but the old woman almost seemed pleased.

"It is a German band," Victoria said. "They know how to play polka music."

"I don't know how to dance," Susanna said.

The two women stared at her, speechless.

"That's fine," Elsa finally managed to say, but without a hint of conviction. "You can learn. Beau can show you."

"The first dance is a traditional dance." Victoria gestured for her to sit on a nearby chair and began to brush her hair.

"A Czech tradition?" Susanna asked.

"Yes, for Czechs, but for many people," Victoria said. "It is called the Grand March. It is an important dance. It shows many things."

Susanna didn't understand how a dance could show many things, but as Victoria explained, she began to grasp what Victoria meant. The parts of the dance represented aspects of marriage.

"In the beginning, the couple holds hands. The music starts, and the couple begin to walk, side-by side. Other couples walk behind them, like a parade, yes?"

Susanna nodded.

"When they get to end of floor, they separate. Because of..." Victoria turned to Elsa. "Because they are..."

"They separate to show disagreement," Elsa said. "But they come back together, right away. Because they want to stop. You know?"

"They want to make up after their argument?" Susanna asked.

"Yes. That's right," Elsa said.

"And then they walk more to end of floor, but this time they continue together, going back to other end of floor. Next time, they join hands with others to dance." Victoria's eyes sparkled. "First, there is one. Then two, Then four. Then eight. To show that their family grows. There are many other small parts of the dance to show life and the marriage. In the end, everyone makes a big circle. The man and wife dance in the middle. The circle is the family and friends and shows that the man and wife have much love. You know? All around them."

Susanna felt a lump in her throat. A surge of emotions washed over her, from where she didn't know. A moment ago, she'd felt fine. Suddenly, she found herself on the verge of tears. The Novak ladies pretended not to notice.

When Susanna recovered, she spoke softly, her voice still tight. "I don't think we can perform your dance, Victoria. How would Beau and I know what to do? It sounds a little bewildering. I wouldn't want to do it wrong."

Elsa shook her head. "Someone will show you. You will follow another couple. It will be fine."

"Who will we follow?" Susanna couldn't think of any of Beau's family that might know a traditional dance.

"You will follow Elsa," Victoria said. "Elsa will lead."

Susanna drew a sharp breath. Elsa was going to lead? Wouldn't that require the solemn widow to dance with a *partner*?

Elsa kept busy, bent over a small tin, searching for hair pins for Susanna's hair. Victoria finished brushing Susanna's hair and set the brush on a nearby table. She motioned for Susanna to get up and helped her into the wedding dress.

Susanna glanced over her shoulder and gave Victoria an inquisitive look.

"Fritz," Victoria said to the unspoken question. "Elsa will dance with Fritz Weber."

Victoria hummed a tune as she buttoned the dress.

Susanna had never heard Victoria hum or sing. She'd certainly never heard her speak of Elsa and Fritz doing anything together, much less a wedding dance. Everything was topsy-turvy. Elsa and Fritz would dance. At *her* wedding. In a few hours, Beau Bailey would be her husband and she would be his wife. It was almost too much to take in.

The morning passed quickly, the details a bit of a blur. Elsa and Victoria seemed to sense her confusion and guided her gently through all the preparations. When she was ready, Noah and his wife, Sarah, came to drive her to the church in Sweet Willow.

They ushered her to a small side room where she was met by Henry, Molly and several others.

215

Henry took her arm in his. Molly took her other arm, weeping loudly. Francine brought her a bouquet to carry. Mr. Weber smiled at her and said something about her dress. Then he escorted Molly to a pew as she sobbed. Victoria lowered Susanna's veil. Elsa fussed over her dress. With a final inspection, they gave a nod of approval and made their way to their seats.

The church was filled with people, to Susanna's astonishment. She recounted Victoria's story of the traditional wedding song, the Grand March, and how the married couple would be surrounded by family and friends. She felt overwhelmed, to think that her circle of family and friends now included what seemed like the entire town of Sweet Willow.

The organ began to play, and music filled the church.

Henry patted her hand. "My dear, dear Susanna, I can't tell you how honored I am to share this moment with you."

"Thank you, Henry. For everything."

Henry nodded. His eyes misted. As they entered the church, her attention was drawn to Beau and, from that moment, her thoughts blurred. Beau held her hands. She said her vows. He cupped her jaw as he kissed her. And in that moment, she was wed.

They shared a meal while Beau told his cousins about meeting Susanna on the train. How she'd wanted no part of him, but he'd persisted. His cousins laughed uproariously. Seth complimented Susanna on her wise response to a rascal like Beau Bailey.

Beau grinned at her and shook his head.

Susanna smiled back, her heart brimming with love for her husband.

The party unfolded in the warm mood of the early evening.

The church hall was filled with lanterns that gave off soft light. Dozens of families sat at the tables lining the outside of the hall. Oscar sat with Noah and Sarah's children. The band arranged their instruments while Victoria and Molly oversaw matters. It didn't look as if it was going well between the two ladies.

Elsa had taken advantage of Victoria's distraction and spoke with Fritz Weber on the other side of the hall. It looked like the two of them had eyes only for each other. Elsa smiled. Fritz looked smitten. It was clear their conversation was going a little better than Victoria and Molly's.

When the band began to warm up their instruments, Beau rose beside her. He held out his hand. She set her hand in his and he helped her to her feet.

"You look pretty. So pretty," he said.

"Thank you. And you look handsome."

"When you walked into the church, I could hardly catch my breath."

"Beau..." She felt her face warm.

"It's true. I'd never imagined a bride could look so beautiful."

He lowered to brush a kiss across her lips. "And now you're all mine."

"Yes. All yours."

Elsa called them to the dance floor where others had already congregated. Beau took her hand and led her to the middle of the gathering. Elsa and Fritz held hands, waiting. Victoria was paired with Henry.

"Well, would you look at that," Beau marveled. "I think Victoria Novak is blushing."

"I think Henry is too," Susanna replied. "I think the two of them are fond of each other."

The music began. The revelers cheered. The crowd drew back to give the wedding couple room to start the procession.

"Well, Mrs. Bailey." Beau lifted her hand to his lips and kissed it. "May I have this dance?"

She nodded. "Yes, I would like very much to share this dance with you, Mr. Bailey."

Epilogue

Victoria

The threat of a late frost had been a worry. Peach blossoms were fragile, and a late cold snap could destroy the entire crop. Victoria had fretted about cold nights and the harm they could cause so late in late March. After the cold burst, she visited the orchard every morning to inspect the small tender flowers.

Henry began going with her, offering his company and whatever help he could. He now lived in the cabin Beau had used. Beau and Susanna stayed with Seth and Laura while their new house was built. Each morning, Henry stood on his porch, waiting for Victoria.

Victoria found she welcomed his companionship. She began to look forward to the morning walks. She and Henry talked about small things. Mostly. Sometimes they spoke of big things. Henry told her he never married out of loyalty to Susanna's mother, and because of his affection for Susanna too. Victoria spoke of marrying young, to a man she didn't love but respected. He was a doctor. He helped many people, often for no pay. Her late husband had a very good name.

"A name is important," Henry said.

"I think so too."

They talked about books and music. They watched with interest as the workmen rebuilt Susanna and Beau's cabin. They visited the donkeys, bringing them small treats.

Henry asked her opinion on matters. No one ever asked her opinion. She mentioned that to Elsa one day. Elsa chuckled and said no one ever had the chance. Victoria was too quick to offer her opinion on most matters before anyone ever asked.

Cheeky girl.

After a few months of morning walks with Henry, Victoria had to admit, if only to herself, that the trees were fine and didn't really need to be checked each morning. The blossoms hadn't frozen. The harvest promised to be very good. And the reason for her trips to the orchard had nothing to do with peaches.

She'd considered telling him she didn't have time to walk, but then something happened that changed everything.

Fritz Weber proposed to Elsa.

After that, Victoria was even more grateful for the morning walks. She was close with Elsa, but obviously couldn't talk with her. Not about this matter.

Who else? Susanna was busy with Beau. The two were in love and expecting a baby in the summer. So, it was Henry who listened patiently and tried to cheer her up.

"It's very hard to lose people," she told him, one morning in early June.

They strolled through the orchard. The peaches were almost ready to pick and perfumed the air with a sweet scent. The tree limbs bowed under the weight of their bounty.

Henry walked with his hands clasped behind his back. "You're not losing anyone. You're gaining a family member. Fritz Weber is a fine man."

"And when she marries, Oscar will go with her. You see, I'm really losing *two* people."

"Victoria, they'll be in Sweet Willow." He smiled. "Not Prague."

She frowned. "I'll be all alone. Even Toby will be gone. And I've just started to like him."

"Ask Fritz for a puppy."

"I don't like puppies," she said grudgingly. "I only like Toby because Oscar loves him."

"Elsa can marry if she wishes. It would be best if you give your blessing."

"I know." She sighed wearily. "I know this."

Henry patted her shoulder to sooth her wounded feelings.

She went on. "I like Fritz. A little. His great-grandmother was Czech. But I don't want him to steal Elsa and Oscar."

Henry chuckled. "Steal Elsa and Oscar?"

She lifted her chin. Even though she knew she was acting petulant, she wouldn't relent. Or change her mind. "And even if he has a Czech relative, he's still *mostly* German."

"Excellent point. We must take care he doesn't steal Elsa, Oscar *and* a bushel of carrots. The scamp."

Victoria waved a dismissive hand, trying very hard not to smile. Henry was the only person who could tease her and make her laugh at her own shortcomings or hard-headedness. She considered telling him that while they were alone in the orchard. Then again, she didn't want to give him the satisfaction while sparks of amusement danced in his eyes.

Later that evening, Victoria went to Elsa who sat alone on the porch swing. "I can see how happy you are."

Elsa flinched as if the words pained her. She paled and her eyes held a look of guilt and distress. She didn't reply. Instead, she looked away, studying some point in the fading light.

221

"I want you to be happy, Elsa. You deserve happiness."

"Fritz is so kind to me. And to Oscar too. I never thought I'd love another man. I didn't *plan* to love another."

Victoria leaned against the railing. "Robert Anderson always said I was too hard on you. He said one day I'd regret it, just like he regretted the things he said to his brother."

"I know you love me, and you love Oscar."

Tears stung Victoria's eyes. "I do. With all my heart. Which is why I must let you go."

Elsa's eyes shone with tears. She rose from the swing and wrapped her arms around Victoria. They stood together in silence for a long moment. The breeze stirred the evening air. Swallows swooped across the evening sky. In the west, the first evening star twinkled.

"But you can't leave Sweet Willow," Victoria said.

"No. Never."

"Promise me."

"I promise."

"Make your plans with Fritz. Get married, Elsa. You are young. You should have a second chance."

"You're not exactly elderly." Elsa straightened and gave her a sheepish smile. "Perhaps you can wear a dress that isn't black."

"One thing at a time, Elsa. One thing at a time."

After Victoria gave her blessing, Elsa and Fritz began their wedding preparations. They picked a day in a few weeks' time, planned a meal and guest list. It would be a small wedding. Victoria was grateful they didn't plan a big, lavish party.

Elsa sewed a new dress for herself, a plain, ivory colored dress. She no longer wore her wedding band, Victoria noticed.

Victoria gave no further thought to Elsa's comment about dresses. She planned to wear a nice, black dress to Elsa's wedding. Then, a few days before the wedding, Oscar brought a box from town and gave it to Victoria. He said Francine Bailey had given it to him and instructed him to deliver it right away.

In the box was a soft, lacy, peach colored dress. Victoria immediately closed the box and tucked it in the top of her wardrobe, out of sight. She prepared her words of thanks in her mind, such a lovely dress, but she could not wear it since it would be disrespectful to her late husband. Even so, several times she pulled the dress out and admired it, especially the lace cuffs, before she gently folded it back up and tucked it out of sight again.

When school ended for the year, Oscar began working at the mercantile. Victoria said little to the boy about the work. After relenting to Elsa's wedding, she didn't want to remind Oscar about studying to be a doctor. At fifteen, he was too young to go to medical school. What was more, she'd begun to doubt his desire to be a doctor.

"Oscar will do well whatever he chooses," Henry said one morning as they picked peaches.

"He's a smart boy. He likes to help Fritz. What can I do?" She plucked a peach and set it in the basket. "Nothing. That's what."

"Would you want to go to a doctor who studied medicine just to make his Babka happy?"

She sighed, not bothering to reply. At times, Henry made her opinions sound foolish, even to her own ears.

"He might not be a very good doctor," Henry said.

"Maybe he would be the very best doctor," she retorted.

Henry smiled.

"Fritz talks about Oscar taking over the store one day."

Henry's brows lifted. "And?"

Victoria considered the idea. While she always wanted Oscar to be a doctor, she could imagine him as a shopkeeper. He enjoyed the work very much. He'd earn a very good living and, best of all, he would remain in Sweet Willow.

"It would be fine," she admitted. "I don't want Fritz to promise Oscar something and disappoint him."

"Right. The cad."

Henry was teasing her again. She didn't know what a cad was, but he clearly was poking fun at her long-held opinions.

She went on. "You never know. He might say all sorts of foolish things. Promises that he won't keep."

The next day, Beau took her and Henry to town to shop at the mercantile. Since Elsa's engagement, Henry had offered his arm to Victoria when they walked. It had been decades since she'd held a man's arm and she was surprised how natural it felt.

It was just another example of Henry's kindness. There were others. Since the engagement, he'd left little bouquets for her tucked in various spots in the house. He left other things as well. Short, humorous notes. A book of French poems. Each little gift was precious to her. She'd smile for days after each gesture. Secretly, she'd begun to think he was the dearest man she'd ever known.

They strolled the walkway to the mercantile. Workmen labored in front of the store, perched on ladders, painting the sign. When Victoria lifted her gaze and read the sign, she stopped abruptly. Henry stopped half a step after and followed her astonished gaze.

The men painted a new name on the sign. Where it had read *Weber Mercantile*, it now had a new name. *Novak – Weber Mercantile*

"Oh my," Henry murmured.

"I can't believe my eyes," Victoria said softly.

"Well, that's a lovely surprise. Can you imagine young Oscar? He must be as proud as can be."

Victoria thought about the sign and marveled at Fritz's gesture. It was remarkable. He and Elsa weren't even married, yet he'd put her son's name on the store. Henry pointed out that Fritz had gone so far as to put Oscar's name before his own.

The morning of the wedding, Victoria rose early and made breakfast. She bathed and heated fresh water for Elsa. She woke Oscar and sent him to feed Susanna and Beau's animals. The morning was a blur of activity. Elsa needed help with her hair. Oscar lost a button from his shirt. The two needed to hurry to be ready when Seth came to pick them up.

Victoria rushed to and fro. She barely noticed Henry when he came to say good morning. Later, when the house was quiet, she found the little bundle of flowers tied with a white ribbon. Henry, her dear Henry...

He'd written a note. On the outside it read: *For the lovely mother of the bride.*

She smiled. Elsa was her daughter-in-law, but Henry knew Victoria felt like Elsa was more like a daughter. She opened the note to find words written in Latin. Her breath caught and she read it again. *Amor Vincit Omnia.*

Victoria blinked back the tears that threatened to fall. Slowly, she turned to her wardrobe and took out the dress. It was stylish, or so it seemed to her. With a basque bodice, three-quarter sleeves, and a draped overskirt, the dress was the same color as the peaches in the orchard. She held it close and looked at her reflection in a nearby mirror.

How long had it been? Very long. She hardly recognized herself.

She lay the dress on the bed and studied it as she debated. Finally, she decided that it was time to put on a new dress. Time for a second chance. It was time she would surprise everyone, most of all herself. A smile tugged at her lips. She imagined Elsa's response and how happy she would be that Victoria had come to her wedding in a dress the color of a summer peach.

Working as quickly as she could, she dressed and fixed her hair in a simple chignon. A pair of new shoes stood in the corner of the armoire. One of the Bailey women was a fairy godmother, she decided with a chuckle.

There was a knock at the door.

Just as she left the room, she stopped to read Henry's note once more. As she ran her fingertip over the Latin words, she spoke softly. "Yes, Henry. I think you are right. Love conquers all."

She slipped off her ring and tucked it in the dresser drawer. She crossed the cabin and opened the door to find Henry. A smile lit his face as he noted her new dress.

"Very pretty."

"Thank you."

"The color is lovely on you, Victoria."

"It is... very bright."

"You look regal." He offered his arm. "Are you ready?"

"Yes, Henry." She gave him an answering smile as she took his arm. "I am ready."

The End

Book One of Copper Creek Mail Order Brides
Mail Order Ruth

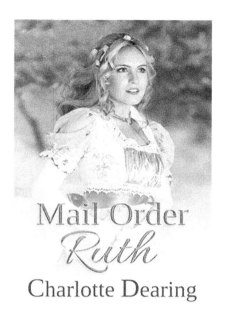

Charlotte Dearing

Gideon searches for a thief. Instead, he finds a jilted mail order bride, two ragged orphans and a basket of striped kittens.

Ruth's been abandoned, but she's still sassy and plenty exasperating. She's taken in a newborn orphan girl and cares for the baby with grit and devotion. Gideon yearns to shelter both Ruth and the sweet baby. He can't make sense of the protective instincts, turning his tidy thoughts all topsy turvy. Before long, he's got more trouble than he can shake a stick at.

Ruth claims to know nothing about the stolen money.
But is she innocent or is she the real thief?

Books by Charlotte Dearing

Sweet Willow Mail Order Brides
Mail Order Abigail
Mail Order Sarah
Mail Order Susanna

Copper Creek Mail Order Brides
Mail Order Ruth
Mail Order Rebecca
Mail Order Holly

The Bluebonnet Brides Collection
Mail Order Grace
Mail Order Rescue
Mail Order Faith
Mail Order Hope
Mail Order Destiny

Brides of Bethany Springs Series
To Charm a Scarred Cowboy
Kiss of the Texas Maverick
Vow of the Texas Cowboy
The Accidental Mail Order Bride
Starry-Eyed Mail Order Bride
An Inconvenient Mail Order Bride
Amelia's Storm

and many others...

Sign up at www.charlottedearing.com to be notified of special offers and announcements.